Breakfast Included

ETERNAL REST
BED AND BREAKFAST

PARANORMAL COZY MYSTERIES

BETH DOLGNER

Breakfast Included
Eternal Rest Bed and Breakfast Book Five
© 2022 Beth Dolgner

All rights reserved. No portion of this book may be reproduced in any form without permission from the publisher, except as permitted by U.S. copyright law.

ISBN-13: 978-1-7365724-9-8

Breakfast Included is a work of fiction. Names, characters, places, and incidents either are the products of the author's imagination or are used fictitiously. Any resemblance to actual persons, living or dead, businesses, companies, events, or locales is entirely coincidental.

Published by Redglare Press
Cover by Dark Mojo Designs
Print Formatting by The Madd Formatter

https://bethdolgner.com

1

The funeral home had given out paper fans. Emily was waving hers frantically toward her face, convinced that hot, humid air that was moving was somehow better than hot, humid air that was stagnant. Her black dress felt stifling under the June sun, and her low black heels were slowly sinking into the perfectly manicured green grass that covered Oak Hill Memorial Garden.

It's hard to feel sad when you're sweating so much.

Emily nearly laughed at the thought, since it was also hard to feel sad when the deceased was someone who had once threatened her with a shotgun. The brief moment of levity was quickly replaced by genuine sadness, not for the man whose coffin sat poised above an open grave, but for the man standing next to it.

Trevor had known his dad didn't have long, since his cancer treatments could only buy him some time, not save his life. Still, the end had come sooner than expected for Mr. Williams, and Emily knew that even though he had once tried to kill his two sons, they were both grieving their loss.

The crowd of black-clad people shifted a little, and Emily briefly got a clear view of Trevor and Dillan Williams. Both of them had their eyes fixed on the casket, their expressions stoic. Their sister, standing between them, had her face buried in a handkerchief.

Emily heard a quiet, impatient sigh to her right, and she glanced over to see her best friend, Sage Clark, fanning herself with equal gusto. Sage, at least, had thought to put on a sun hat, though she had explained to Emily it wasn't for sun protection as much as it was to hide her pink, spiked hair. "There's going to be enough gossip about this funeral without people being shocked over my hair color!" Sage had quipped.

Sage leaned toward Emily and whispered, "I'm hot, and I'm hungry! Is this preacher ever going to wrap things up?"

Emily simply responded with a little shrug, but she was feeling as impatient as Sage. The service at the church had been a long one, and Emily had gotten the impression the preacher hoped he could make up for the bad things Benjamin Williams had done in life by talking longer than usual. Apparently, he didn't feel like he'd talked quite enough yet, because the graveside service was lasting an unusually long time, too.

After another ten minutes, during which Emily only caught about half of what the preacher actually said, since she was so far back in the crowd of people, the casket was lowered on ropes into the ground, and the funeral was over.

"Finally!" Sage said, loudly enough that a few people nearby threw disapproving glances in her direction. "Jen suggested we go get salads at The Depot for lunch. It's too hot for cooked food!"

"I'm in," Emily said. "I just want to say hello to Trevor and Dillan before we go."

"Oh, of course," Jen chimed in. "We want to offer our condolences, too." Jen's red hair was pulled up in a French twist, and paired with her well-tailored black dress, she looked like she belonged at a cocktail party instead of a funeral. Only the beads of sweat across her forehead ruined the illusion.

Sage yawned widely, then said, "Remember old Mr. Thatcher? He's the guy who owned the barbershop on the square for about fifty years. He came to the funeral, too!"

"My dad was devastated when Mr. Thatcher retired," Emily said. "He claims he hasn't had a decent haircut since. I wonder if he used to cut Mr. Williams's hair, too?"

"That would be my guess. Mr. Thatcher died, what, ten years ago or so? My dad went to him, too." Sage looked toward the edge of the crowd and gave a little wave. Emily couldn't see Mr. Thatcher's ghost, but she knew Sage saw him almost as if he were just another funeral-goer.

"Are there a lot of ghosts here?" Emily asked.

"No, not a lot. I find cemeteries to be less haunted than most people expect them to be."

"All right, let's work our way up there," Jen said. She took Sage's hand and began moving forward, snaking her way among the knots of people who were talking together. As she followed, Emily looked around at the sea of faces. She recognized many of them since she had lived in Oak Hill, Georgia, her entire life. She wondered how many of the people were there to honor Mr. Williams, and how many of them were there simply to gawk at the spectacle. It wasn't every day the small town had a funeral for a convicted murderer.

I'll have to tell Kelly about this and ask her what she thinks of it. Kelly Stern had been Dillan's girlfriend when the two of them were teenagers, and Mr. Williams had killed her years ago. Her restless ghost had remained behind, hoping to get justice one day. Once Kelly's ghost had helped bring the details of her murder to light, though, she had opted to remain at Eternal Rest Bed and Breakfast with Emily and the house's other resident ghosts.

There was already a long line of people waiting to talk to the Williams siblings, so instead, Emily headed toward her friend Reed Marshall, who was standing nearby. His dark-green suit looked expensive, and it perfectly set off his dark skin and eyes. Before she could stop herself, Emily blurted, "You look so handsome!"

One side of Reed's mouth turned up in a little smile, and he winked at Emily. "Thank you. I know I do, because three women have already given me their phone number."

"Seriously? At a funeral?"

"You'd be surprised how often it happens." Reed shrugged good-naturedly. "A lot of people come to funerals because they have to, not because they want to. They're not grieving, and they know I'm not, either, since I'm just the sexton."

Emily let the information sink in for a few moments, then said, "Are you going to call any of them?"

Reed chuckled quietly. "No. I don't date where I dig."

"Nice line." Emily rolled her eyes, though she failed to look very disapproving since she was also trying not to laugh. "Speaking of lines, I'd better go get in the one for Trevor and Dillan. I don't want to keep Sage and Jen waiting."

Emily joined the line, and after just a few minutes, she was extending her hand to Dillan Williams. His dark-blond hair and beard were neatly trimmed, though his green eyes looked tired.

Dillan took Emily's proffered hand, then abruptly let go and wrapped his arms around Emily in a tight hug. "Thank you for coming," he said, his voice cracking. "You and Sage know better than anyone in this town how little my dad deserves this fanfare, and I know you're really here for me and Trevor."

Emily felt her throat tighten. "You have my support and my condolences." It felt like such a generic thing to say, but in that moment, Emily couldn't think of anything else. Still, it seemed to be enough for Dillan, who relaxed his arms and gave Emily a grateful smile.

The next person in line was Trevor and Dillan's sister, whom Emily had never met. Emily shook her hand, said a few kind words, then stepped toward Trevor.

Trevor was just saying goodbye to the man who had been going down the line in front of Emily, and when Trevor turned his blue eyes toward hers, Emily felt her chest tighten in sympathy for her friend. Trevor's eyes were red from crying, and he wiped at his tanned face self-consciously. Emily knew Trevor had moved back to Oak Hill to take care of his dad, and even after his arrest—even after trying to kill his own sons—Trevor had continued to show his dad love and forgiveness.

Emily bit her lip as she felt tears of her own beginning to well up. She had talked to Trevor several times since his dad's death a few days before, but between his family obligations and her busy schedule at Eternal Rest, this was the first time she had actually seen him. Instead of trying to say anything, Emily simply reached up and wrapped her arms around Trevor. He knew how well she understood grief, and there was no point in trying to say it in that moment.

"Thank you for coming, Emily," Trevor said softly. He gave a sad laugh. "At least this time, it's not a murder for you to solve!"

Emily turned her head so Trevor's sister wouldn't see her little smile. She appreciated Trevor's attempt at humor, and she knew it was probably a nice distraction for him. She answered quietly, "For *us* to solve, you mean! I'll talk to you soon, okay? Maybe you and Dillan can come over to my house one night for dinner."

"He's heading back Thursday morning."

"So soon? It's already Tuesday! Well, you can come over one night, then, if you like. My guests will be doing some ghost hunting in my cemetery tomorrow night, but after that, I'm up for cooking."

"Sounds good."

Emily gave Trevor one last squeeze and waved as she moved away, heading toward Sage and Jen, who were now talking to Reed. As she approached, Emily saw a woman in a surprisingly slinky dress for such a somber occasion sidle up to Reed and lean in to whisper something to him. Emily caught the flash of a white business card before the woman walked away, looking pleased with herself.

"Another one?" Emily asked, not even bothering to hide her smile this time.

Reed straightened his shoulders proudly. "What can I say? Ladies are *dying* to meet me."

Jen and Sage groaned in unison as Emily waved her hands and said, "No! That's two terrible jokes you've made today. No more funeral humor!"

Reed smiled. "Sorry. I've had to be so composed all morning, so now I'm letting off steam—decomposing, you could say—by telling sexton jokes. They're like dad jokes, but much more grave."

"Oh, that's it," Sage said, one hand over her mouth to stifle her laughter. "We're going to lunch, now. Reed, talk to us when you're back to normal!"

As Sage and Jen turned toward the line of parked cars snaking along the main road through the cemetery, Emily caught Sage's arm. "Do you two mind going ahead to get a table? I'll be there shortly."

"Of course we don't mind," Sage said, "but tell Scott you can't linger too long, because your friends are starving!"

Emily promised to be quick, then turned and walked in

the opposite direction. She didn't really like Oak Hill Memorial Garden, but she was especially critical of it when she was hot and sweaty. The wide expanse of lawn was peppered with only a few trees, so there was no shade to provide relief as Emily walked to Scott's grave. She knew her late husband's spirit wasn't there. Instead, it was trapped outside a mysterious psychic barrier that surrounded the town, but Emily still felt comfort in visiting his burial spot.

"Hey, Scott," Emily said as she walked up to the low granite marker that read *Scott Buchanan, Beloved Husband and Son*. "Sage and Jen send their love. I was so relieved to see your ghost last month, and I know we're getting closer to being able to help you. Kelly says she's spotted you a few times since then and that you're looking stronger. That's great! You'd be happy with how busy things have been at Eternal Rest. I've got another new assistant: Trish's boy, Clint. Remember him? He's grown up a lot, and he's already been working for me for two weeks. So far, he's doing great. Well, I can't stay long. For one thing, I think I'm going to melt if I don't get somewhere air-conditioned soon! For another, I'm meeting Sage and Jen at The Depot for lunch. Oh! Before I go, you should know that I—"

Emily cut off abruptly as a woman screamed. Several people began running toward the sound, and Emily's eyes followed them as they dashed toward the woman in the slinky dress who had given Reed her number. Her hands were clutching her face, and her mouth was open in an expression of horror.

"He's dead!" she shrieked.

Well, of course he's dead, Emily thought, even as she realized the woman wasn't looking at the grave of Benjamin Williams. The woman pointed toward the ground and wailed, "There's a dead body!"

Emily began to run toward the woman, even as her mind told her not to get involved in what might be yet another murder.

Your life has been murder-free for a whole month, she lectured herself. *Don't go over there!*

But it was too late. The last of the funeral guests were all crowding around the woman who had screamed, and Emily had nearly reached the onlookers already. She came up behind two men and peered through the small gap between them. There was an open grave there, the dirt piled to one side in a haphazard fashion. The woman was pointing into the grave, and Emily speculated that was where the body must be.

Instinctively, Emily took a step back. She didn't want to see what was in that hole in the ground. After discovering the body of one of her guests not long ago, she didn't feel the need to see any more fresh corpses.

The open grave wasn't far from where the graveside service for Mr. Williams had been held, but it was easy to see why it had gone unnoticed for so long. It was screened by tall shrubs that surrounded a bench and a fountain. Reed's admirer had simply been unfortunate enough to wander off in the wrong direction.

If Scott had been buried over that way, it would have been me who found the body.

Reed's voice cut through the babble. "Everybody, please step back! This is a crime scene, so you need to keep your distance! We are calling the police right now."

Emily looked toward Reed, and she saw how grim his expression was. Reed was the sexton of both this cemetery and the historic Hilltop Cemetery next to Emily's house. Reed dealt with dead bodies all the time, but not quite like this.

The crowd of onlookers had barely moved, despite Reed's request, and he raised his voice again. "Please, head on home. Sabrina here will stay to give her statement to the police, but the rest of you should clear out so you don't interfere with any evidence."

Sabrina, Emily noticed, now had her arms around Reed, her head buried in his shoulder.

Slowly, reluctantly, the crowd moved away from the open grave, though they all gathered a short distance away, clearly anxious to watch the spectacle and not at all interested in leaving. Emily took a few steps back as the men screening her view walked away, but she called Reed's name loudly. "Do you want me to stay and help?" she asked as he looked up.

Reed shook his head. "No, go have lunch. You've had enough to deal with lately."

Emily gave him a look that she hoped conveyed her sympathy for the awful turn his day had just taken, then began walking toward her car. As she passed by some of the onlookers, she overheard a man say, "It's Thornton Daley. Did you see how purple his face looked?"

"I'm going to have nightmares for a month," replied his companion. "I wonder who killed him?"

"Probably a local restaurant owner. His reviews were

always scathing, and I expect someone finally had enough of it."

Emily actually stopped and turned to the first man. "Is it really Thornton Daley? The food reviewer for *The Oak Hill Monitor*?"

The man nodded, his expression almost gleeful. "It sure is. I used to sell advertising for the paper, and I'd recognize that face anywhere."

Emily just gave a little nod and continued on to her car. As she drove downtown to The Depot, she thought about what she had overheard. Thornton had been the newspaper's food reviewer for years, and he had a reputation around town for being the kind of guy who always found fault with a dish, no matter how good it was. Or, if he wasn't upset with the food itself, then he would find a reason to criticize the restaurant's staff, the decor, or—in one notoriously bad review—the fact it was rainy and cold outside, as if the restaurant had been at fault for not providing a nice, sunny day.

If the only suspects in Thornton's murder were disgruntled restaurant owners, Emily realized, then even that list would take the police days to work through.

Jen and Sage were seated at a table inside The Depot, and Emily could tell by all the other black-clad diners that a lot of people had gone straight from the cemetery to lunch. Before Emily could even sit down, Sage announced, "Someone found a body at the cemetery!"

"I know. I was there when she found it, but how do you know already?" Emily sank down into her chair, feeling drained after the heat and emotion of the morning.

Sage made a dismissive gesture. "Phone calls go faster than your car. Someone already called a friend who's here, and that person must have told Jay, and so, of course, everyone in the whole place already knows."

Emily nodded knowingly. Jay, the owner of The Depot,

was one of the best sources of gossip in Oak Hill. "I didn't care for Thornton Daley, but it's a shame he's dead," Emily said.

"Oh!" Jen leaned forward. "It's him? Most of the restaurants in town are members of the Chamber of Commerce, and at every business mixer we host, I get to hear them complaining about how Thornton has it out for them. He is—er, was—so unpopular."

"I didn't actually see the body, but one of the men who did told me it was Thornton. He said they used to work together. You know that lady who came up to flirt with Reed while we were talking to him? She's the one who found him. Apparently, the body was dumped in an open grave."

"Did someone kill him at the cemetery, or did they take his body there to bury it? And if they wanted to bury him, why is he in an open grave?" Jen's eyes were wide.

"Those are good questions, but I don't have the answers," Emily said. "Hopefully, the police can sort this one out without me or my ghosts getting involved. Or Sage, for that matter."

Sage looked at Emily keenly. "You're implying that you think his ghost is still around, and Detective Hernandez might want me to communicate with it. Did you sense anything at the cemetery?"

"No. I was talking to Scott when the woman started screaming about a body. I was too shocked to even think about whether Thornton's ghost was there." Emily sighed deeply and leaned back in her chair as a server approached the table.

After ordering, Sage picked right back up with, "I hope our services aren't needed, too. I can't seem to sleep enough to stop feeling tired all the time. I've started blocking off an hour of my afternoon schedule every day so I can take a nap on the couch at my shop!"

"You and I should both cross our fingers that Thornton Daley has gone on to the great restaurant in the sky," Emily answered.

By the time Emily pulled into the driveway of Eternal Rest Bed and Breakfast, she felt like her fingers could barely grip the steering wheel. The funeral alone had been emotionally draining, since not only did she feel sorrow for Trevor and Dillan, but it inevitably made her think of Scott's funeral more than two years before.

Witnessing the moment someone discovered a dead body only added to her exhaustion. On top of that, the entire month of June had nearly passed, but it felt like a blur. Eternal Rest had been booked every single night that month, and Emily was worn out from the constant cleaning, accompanying guests to the cemetery next door for nighttime ghost hunting, and having almost zero time to herself.

Emily walked through the back door of the old Victorian home, the wooden floorboards of the hallway creaking out a welcome as she headed toward the parlor. The silence of the house told her that her guests were still out sightseeing.

Clint Alden was sitting at the rolltop desk situated in a back corner of the parlor. He was swiveling slowly back and forth in the chair, his eyes fixed on the screen of his cell phone. Without looking up, he said, "Hi, Emily. Did you see him?"

"See who?"

"That dead newspaper guy." Clint looked up this time, his light-brown hair catching the light streaming through the windows. "My friend's cousin was at the funeral."

Emily laughed. "You're like your mama, you know. She's always up on the latest gossip, too!"

Clint shrugged easily. "Not much else to do in this town."

"How has your day been?"

"Good. I booked a party who wants to stay here during Halloween, and I ran the dishwasher for you. It didn't seem fair to make you clean up from breakfast after being at a funeral all morning."

"Thank you so much, Clint," Emily said with feeling. Clint's job as her assistant was to field phone calls, fulfill reservation requests, and generally keep an eye on the house when she wasn't there. The fact he had taken it upon himself to do some cleaning was touching. Clint was heading into his senior year of high school in the fall, and Emily was happy to see what a thoughtful son her friend Trish and her husband had raised.

Emily hesitated a moment, then said, "I'm actually going to take a quick nap. Since I cleaned the guest rooms before I left this morning, I think I can get a little rest in. You good here?"

Clint gave Emily a thumbs up and a big smile. "All good!"

Emily retreated to her bedroom, which was just behind the parlor. She changed into sweatpants and a T-shirt, relieved to be out of her dress and heels, before falling into bed. She snuggled under the covers, sighed, and fell asleep instantly.

It was a knock at her bedroom door that brought Emily out of a deep sleep. She blinked a few times, feeling groggy, then got up and shuffled to the door. Clint stood there, looking slightly worried. "It's a little after five o'clock, so I'm heading out," he said.

Emily felt a jolt as her weariness disappeared, replaced by surprise. "Five? I slept for almost three hours? Oh, wow,

I knew I was tired, but... Thanks for waking me up. Has your mom been by yet?"

"Not yet. That's one of the reasons I wanted to make sure you were awake. She texted that she'll be here a little before six."

"Okay. Have a good night, Clint. I'll see you Thursday."

Once Clint was gone, Emily quickly got dressed in her usual uniform of black jeans and a dark-blue button-down shirt that had *Eternal Rest Bed and Breakfast* embroidered in silver on the left breast. She also ran a brush through her hair before twisting it into a low bun.

The house was still quiet, and Emily breathed a sigh of relief that her guests weren't back yet, since it wouldn't look professional if they returned to find their hostess fast asleep. She knew she had been tired, but she hadn't realized just how much she needed to let her body and brain rest. Emily felt a wave of gratitude that Clint had agreed to come work for her on Tuesdays and Thursdays, giving her a little bit of peace during such a chaotic summer.

Emily made herself a pot of coffee before heading back to the parlor. As she set a steaming mug down on the rolltop desk, she noticed the blank sheet of paper she kept next to her laptop was now covered in Kelly Stern's looping handwriting. *Saw him today! Looking better than ever!* The note was followed by a big smiley face with hearts for eyes.

3

Kelly had seen Scott's ghost beyond the barrier.

While a lot of ghosts seemed to prefer communicating through sound—whether that meant knocking on a wall, speaking on ghost hunters' tape recorders, or similar methods—Kelly liked to write messages. Kelly never wrote if Emily was looking at the sheets of paper she left in various spots throughout the downstairs rooms, but Emily always knew it was Kelly by the teenager's swooping style of writing and her copious use of exclamation points.

Emily looked around the room, knowing Kelly was present but not exactly where she might be. "Thank you, Kelly! I'm so glad to hear it!"

Between the nap and the good news that Scott's ghost seemed to be getting stronger and easier to see, Emily felt energized. By the time Trish stopped by with breakfast goods from Grainy Day Bakery, Emily was humming to herself while she responded to emails. As Emily had expected, Trish was brimming with gossip about the funeral and the discovery of the body. Emily admitted she had been there when it happened, and Trish's eyes got wider and wider as Emily told her the details.

Emily's guests returned to Eternal Rest just a few minutes after Trish had left. The group of six were ghost hunters from Indiana, and they were staying for a full week. They had just checked in the day before, and Emily found them to be a congenial group.

Originally, like so many of her guests, the group simply wanted to conduct their paranormal investigations at the house and at Hilltop Cemetery next door. Just a day before, though, a local florist had called Emily, asking if she had any ghost hunters staying at Eternal Rest who might want to come investigate at her shop. After never having anything odd happen, the florist explained, vases were suddenly being pushed off the shelves or simply moving from one place to another when no one was present. Emily's guests had enthusiastically accepted the invitation to investigate there, and they were scheduled to be at the shop by eight o'clock that night.

"We came back to change into our team T-shirts and to load up our gear," said Marlon, the one who had booked the reservation and seemed to be in charge of the ghost-hunting activities. "Thanks again for setting this up for us!"

"No problem," Emily said. "Y'all are going to help Etta-Jane get some answers and, hopefully, keep the vases safe from any more spectral shenanigans! Hang on a second." Emily dug through the top drawer of her desk, finally pulling out a key. "Here's a spare key for the front door, since I'll likely be in bed by the time you get back tonight. Like we discussed earlier, I'll have breakfast out at nine instead of the usual seven."

As Marlon retreated upstairs to get ready for the night's ghost hunting, the phone rang. When Emily answered, she heard nothing for several seconds. Then, she heard a deep male voice say, "Hi."

Emily waited for more, but when the silence returned, she prompted, "May I help you?"

"Is this Emily?"

"It is."

"Hi, Emily. I don't believe we've met. My name is Aaron Calloway. I'm the principal at Oak Hill High School. I ran into Etta-Jane, and she said you have some ghost hunters going to her flower shop tonight."

"Yes, that's right." Emily was sitting straight up in her chair, curious where this strange conversation was heading.

"Well, you see, I, uh…"

Emily recognized the hesitant tone. "Let me guess: you have a haunting you need help with, too?"

Aaron laughed self-consciously. "It's just that I've never really believed in any of this stuff. We've never had anything strange at the school, but over the past month or so, I started hearing students talk about locker doors banging open on their own, lights flickering, even strange noises coming from the auditorium. You know how teenagers are: they're always telling urban legends and trying to scare each other silly. I didn't believe any of it, of course."

Aaron paused again, but this time, Emily stayed silent, knowing he would continue the tale when he was ready. "We don't use the entire campus during summer school. One of my maintenance guys was working in an empty classroom two weeks ago, and he heard banging in the hallway. He walked out, and every single locker door was wide open. No one was in sight. Then, last Friday, I went to the auditorium. I heard voices coming from the stage, but no one was in there with me. Every door was locked, and I searched every nook and cranny in case someone was hiding. I promise you, it wasn't anyone playing a prank."

"That's weird," Emily said, more to herself than to Aaron.

"That I'm hearing voices?"

"No, I mean it's weird the high school is suddenly haunted, just like the florist is. And Jay started having problems at The Depot about a month ago. My friend Sage works in a building just off the square, and she said something has started haunting the hallway outside her office. Why are all these ghosts popping up all of a sudden?"

"I don't know, but I don't like it. Do you think your guests would like to check out the high school?"

"I think they'll be thrilled to investigate there. I'm supposed to be taking them to the cemetery next door tomorrow night. What about Thursday evening? I can ask them if that would work."

"Thank you, Emily. I'm hoping we can take care of this problem before school starts in the fall."

Emily wanted to tell Aaron hauntings weren't usually problems; they were simply something one had to learn to live with. The activity he was describing at the high school didn't sound at all dangerous. Still, she could understand how the sudden paranormal activity might be unsettling, especially for a skeptic, and scary to any students who witnessed it. Emily wrote down Aaron's phone number and promised to call him back once she had talked to her guests.

She didn't have long to wait. Marlon and three of the other guests came downstairs half an hour later, each carrying a black case full of what Emily assumed was ghost-hunting equipment. The four of them marched out the front door to load everything into their three vehicles, then returned to the house. Emily was waiting for them in the hallway, and when she told them about Aaron's request, all four began nodding enthusiastically.

"Is this normal for your guests to have so many investigation requests?" Marlon asked.

"Not in the slightest," Emily answered. "Maybe you can ask the ghost at the florist why it's suddenly acting up."

Marlon promised the team would ask, then Emily let them return to their work while she called Aaron back.

Soon, the entire group of guests was in the hallway, ready to head out for the night. Emily came out of the parlor to see them off, telling them to have fun and be safe.

Once her guests were on their way, Emily stepped onto the wide front porch and leaned against a column, enjoying the soft evening breeze. The western horizon beyond Hilltop Cemetery still glowed with the last bit of daylight. As a child, Emily had loved the long days of summer, reveling in the extra time she could spend outside playing. Now that she was an adult, the daylight made her feel less lonely.

"Are you out there now, Scott?" Emily asked, squinting at the sky above the hill the cemetery was built on. She thought about going to the bench on the far side of the cemetery, where she had seen Scott's ghost a month before. As she debated whether it was even worth it, since Scott hadn't appeared to her since that one night, her cell phone rang.

Emily didn't recognize the number on the caller ID, but it was the local area code. "Hello?"

"Hi, Emily, this is Britney over at Oak Hill Sport and Leisure."

Emily had been in the sporting goods store before, but she couldn't imagine why someone from there would be calling her.

Unless… No, it can't be. Not another one!

But it was, and Emily instinctively knew it. She said frankly, "What sort of paranormal activity are you having, Britney?"

"How did you know?" Britney sounded surprised, and Emily could just picture her expression.

"You're not the first to call with a sudden haunting. It seems like ghosts around Oak Hill are—I don't know—waking up or something."

"Yeah. Three times in the past month, I've come in to

open up in the morning and found things messed up. Golf clubs laid end-to-end around the store, soccer balls shoved into the trash can, and, today, every single hiking and camping book had been thrown onto the floor. I was telling Trish about it when I went to her place for a bagel, and she said I should call you. Hope you don't mind she gave me your number."

"Not at all. I'll be honest with you, though: my current guests are starting to get a crowded calendar because of the other people who have been calling and asking for help. I'll talk to them, though."

"But if they can't come out, your next guests can, right?" Britney sounded frustrated, and again, Emily had to remind herself that even a harmless haunting could feel like a big problem to someone who wasn't used to coexisting with ghosts.

"I don't believe my next group of guests is a paranormal investigation team, but I'll double-check and let you know. I'll call you back after I've had a chance to look at upcoming reservations. I promise I'll have ghost hunters here with me soon enough."

Britney thanked Emily three times before hanging up. Emily leaned over and put her elbows on the porch railing. What was going on? Why were hauntings suddenly popping up all over Oak Hill?

As if in answer to her silent questions, a loud, metallic banging echoed from the direction of the cemetery.

It wasn't the first time Emily had heard the loud noise. Previously, it had sounded as if an angry fist were pounding against the iron door of a mausoleum, but this time the noise seemed both louder and longer. Emily peered toward the sea of headstones and mausoleums, trying to spot any people or other things roaming across the hill. She saw nothing out of the ordinary.

As the echoes of the banging sound faded away, Emily could hear the crickets chirping and the leaves of the trees softly dancing in the breeze. She stood still for a while, trying to reach out with her mind, but she didn't sense anything. If there was a ghost in the cemetery who was responsible for all the racket, then Emily couldn't detect its presence. She chided herself for how little she had been practicing her growing mediumship abilities. Sage reminded her on a regular basis to meditate with her Tarot cards or to try new ways of sensing and communicating with the ghosts of Eternal Rest, but Emily had just been too busy to properly apply herself.

Emily didn't hear any other strange noises in the next few minutes, so she finally retreated into the house. She made dinner before taking her laptop to bed so she could watch some old TV shows to help distract her from the day's draining experiences. She eventually fell asleep while thinking it had been the longest Tuesday of her life.

The ghost hunters returned shortly after two o'clock in the morning. Emily woke up to hear them all treading quietly up the stairs. Before she fell back to sleep, she was surprised at how relieved she felt to no longer be alone in the house. Between the funeral, the body in the open grave, and the strange noise in the cemetery, Emily had to admit she was feeling a little overwhelmed, and maybe even a little spooked.

It was rare for Emily to sleep past her usual wake-up time of six o'clock, but she managed to do it on Wednesday morning, despite her long nap the day before. She got out of bed at eight instead, when her alarm told her it was time to get up and make breakfast.

Two of Emily's guests, a couple named Louis and Janie, were the first ones downstairs. Both of them found Emily in the parlor to thank her for setting up the investigation at the florist. They promised the group would fill her in on how it went as soon as they had eaten breakfast.

Emily didn't have to wait long before she was called into the dining room. Her guests regaled her with the story of seeing a vase fly across the room on its own before smashing against a wall. Instead of being scared by the experience, all six of them were excited. After they finished telling her about their night, Emily told them about hers. Since the group would be looking for ghosts at Hilltop Cemetery that night, they were enthusiastic about trying to track down the source of the sound Emily had heard.

No sooner had Emily returned to the parlor than her cell phone began to ring. Seeing it was her mom calling, Emily steeled herself for a barrage of questions. She knew the news of Thornton Daley's death had reached her mother, and Rayna Ward would want to know every detail.

Rayna didn't even return Emily's greeting. Instead, she

said excitedly, "Emily, what was it like? The newspaper article barely has any detail, of course, but I know you went to the funeral for that awful man yesterday, so you must have seen something!"

Emily quickly filled her mother in, though Rayna seemed disappointed Emily had made the conscious choice not to look at the body.

"The article said the cause of death was still unknown," her mom said after Emily concluded. "Of course, they probably had to go to press just hours after the whole thing happened, so hopefully tomorrow's paper will have more detail. Do you think he was murdered?"

"Maybe he knew he was dying of natural causes, so he flung himself into an open grave to save his family the effort and expense of a traditional burial," Emily answered sarcastically.

"Emily, we're talking about a dead man. This is serious."

Emily actually laughed. "So it's okay to gossip about him, but it's not okay to joke about him?"

"Well…" Rayna gave a self-conscious chuckle. "You have a point."

"I'm sure you'll learn a lot more from whatever the newspaper reports tomorrow than from me. My goal is to stay as far away from this murder as possible!"

"Good. You need a break from bodies. I'll call you if I hear any other bits of news!"

Emily shook her head as she wished her mom a good morning and hung up. While she did feel some curiosity about Thornton Daley's death, she wasn't nearly as eager as Rayna to know all the gruesome details.

Once breakfast was cleaned up, Emily had some time on her hands as her guests returned to their rooms to get ready for the day. She walked to Hilltop Cemetery, passing through the ornate wrought-iron gate as she kept a lookout for Reed. Halfway up the path that led from the gate to the top of the hill that had given the cemetery its name, Emily spied him and his team on a path that led to the left.

Reed looked much different than he had at the funeral, but it was the version of him Emily was used to seeing. He was wearing blue jeans and a black sweatshirt. As Emily approached, Reed had his gloved hands clamped around the top of an old headstone as two of the men on his team carefully adjusted the position of its base. When they finished, Reed said something quietly to them, then looked up at Emily. "This headstone had been broken clean in two. My guys did a great job restoring it, didn't they?"

"It looks fantastic!" Emily enthused. The inscription on the stone had weathered over the years, but she could clearly see the date of 1891 on it.

Reed stepped toward Emily, his voice lower. "You doing okay?"

"Me? I'm fine! I was coming to check on you!"

Reed swept his arm toward the rows of graves nearest them. "I work with the dead, so yesterday wasn't hard for me. Granted, I don't expect fresh dead bodies to just magically appear in graves, but it certainly wasn't as shocking for me as it was for everyone else who saw him."

"Do you know what killed him?" Emily almost laughed at herself. After chiding her mother for being so interested in the murder, she was now doing the same thing.

"No. I'm sure they're doing an autopsy today, so we'll know soon enough." Reed looked at Emily keenly, then added, "I have no idea who might have killed him, either."

"How did you know that was my next question?"

Reed simply smiled mysteriously at Emily. Even though she regularly accused him of being more tuned in to the unseen world than he admitted, Emily expected this wasn't a case of Reed having some supernatural flash of insight. Instead, every single other person Reed talked to was probably asking him the same questions. That thought reminded Emily she had another question for Reed. "Have you heard any loud banging sounds here at Hilltop?" she asked abruptly. "I mean that metallic sound I've mentioned to you before."

"I haven't, but if you've heard it again, then it's probably just a ghost." Like bodies, Reed had an unusually casual attitude about ghosts.

"None of the longtime ghosts here have ever done something like that. So does that mean one of them is acting up for some reason, or do I have a new ghost here? And if I have a new ghost, where did they come from? There haven't been new burials here for years." Emily gave an exasperated sigh.

"Don't forget, Kelly's ghost was here for years, but she didn't start actively haunting until I found her necklace," Reed pointed out. "Maybe something has changed here in the cemetery, and the energetic shift has stirred up a dormant ghost. Maybe the work my team and I do is responsible. It sounds to me like some of your guests, or maybe you and Sage, need to come here and do some spirit communication."

"My guests are investigating here tonight. Hopefully, they'll learn something useful. All right, now that I know you're not traumatized after yesterday's discovery, I'm heading back to clean rooms. Keep me posted, Reed!" Emily waved at him and his team before walking back down the hill.

Emily's guests were just leaving for a day of exploring Oak Hill as she returned, so she immediately got to work cleaning their rooms. With that done, it was time to dust and sweep the downstairs, then catch up on reservation requests.

The day passed quickly, and Emily was a little surprised when Trish arrived with the baked goods for the next morning's breakfast. It didn't feel like it should be nearly six o'clock already, especially when the day before had seemed to last so long. Emily opened the door to find Trish looking a little frazzled. Wisps of blonde hair had escaped her French braid, and there was a big spot of flour on her Grainy Day Bakery shirt.

"Hey, Trish. What's going on?"

Trish reached out with a bag and two boxes of baked goods in her hands, but her eyes seemed focused on something far away. With a little shake of her head, she snapped her gaze to Emily. "Hey, Emily," Trish answered in her thick Southern accent. "I think I have a ghost at my bakery!"

"Oh! Another one?" Emily took the baked goods out of Trish's hands and placed them carefully on the floor behind her, then quickly turned her attention back to Trish. The last time Trish had a ghost, it had been a murder victim haunting an antique mirror. Fortunately, the killer had been identified not long after, and the ghost had crossed over, satisfied that justice had been done. Unfortunately, Emily had been forced to break the mirror to help release the ghost. A month had passed since then, but she still felt bad about destroying such a beautiful antique, and she repeated her apologies to Trish regularly.

Trish nodded emphatically. "Yeah, and it makes what happened with that mirror seem like nothing! At least the mirror didn't impede on my baking. It just shouted and moved around on its own. This morning, when I walked in, I found that my fridge had been unplugged. I didn't think it was paranormal—I mean, things happen, right?—but then, an hour after I'd plugged it back in, there the cord was, lying right across the floor like something was trying to draw my attention to it."

Emily opened her mouth to respond as Trish took a deep breath, but she wasn't finished yet. "It happened three more times during the day. And, while I was making the dough for tomorrow morning, my mixer suddenly stopped. I'm sure you won't be surprised when I tell you it was unplugged, too. Later, my oven was turned off while I had croissants in to bake."

This time, Trish actually was finished with her narrative. Emily leaned against the doorframe and crossed her arms. She gazed over Trish's shoulder to the woods on the other side of the road, thinking.

"Well? What do you think?" Trish finally prompted.

"Have you talked to Jay lately? He's got a new haunting at The Depot. The same goes for the florist, the high school, the athletic store on the square… The list goes on."

Trish chewed on her lip nervously. "Where are all these ghosts coming from? Or have they always been around, but something has gotten them all stirred up?"

Emily finally pulled her eyes away from the trees and looked at Trish. "I've been asking the same questions. Even Sage doesn't know what's happening. She's been so busy lately that by the time she wraps up with work, she's too drained to go chasing after all the new ghosts."

"I'm not a psychic medium," Trish said, "but I was raised by parents who believe in ghosts, and they always taught me to trust my instincts. Whatever is going on in Oak Hill may or may not have something to do with the strange activity at my bakery, but I can tell you this: I got the feeling that whatever kept unplugging things wanted to keep me from doing my work. It was like it was trying to stop me by cutting the power to every appliance I rely on to bake."

Like Trish, Emily couldn't imagine why any ghost would want to prevent her from baking. While some of the other paranormal activity happening around Oak Hill was strange, none of it seemed designed to keep someone from making their living. Even the florist, who had to deal with vases getting broken, had admitted it felt more like a ghost letting off some steam rather than any kind of malice directed toward her.

Once Trish left to go home, Emily had plenty to keep her mind busy while she waited for her ghost hunters to return from town. She made dinner early, knowing they would want to get set up in the cemetery as soon as it got dark.

In just a few short hours, Emily found herself in Hilltop once again, this time simply supervising her guests as they prepared to investigate in front of the mausoleum perched at the very top of the hill. The ornate granite structure resembled a tiny Greek temple, complete with columns across the front, and it was the final resting place of Oak Hill's first mayor. Even though Emily had told Marlon no one had ever reported paranormal activity there, she had also admitted no ghost hunters had ever tried looking for ghosts at that spot.

After setting up their video cameras, tape recorders,

and a machine that projected a grid of thousands of laser points across the front of the mausoleum—in order to detect any shadows or movement in the dark, Marlon explained—the team sat down and began trying to communicate with the mayor or whomever else might be present.

Emily liked to accompany her guests to the cemetery when they went after hours, more to ensure their safety than out of fear they might do any harm. There were plenty of uneven walkways and wayward tree roots that could result in a sprained ankle or worse. Once her guests were seated and working, Emily wandered to the far side of the mausoleum so she could gaze toward the faint glow on the horizon that indicated the next town over.

It was from a nearby bench that Emily had looked at that same spot and seen the faint, glowing outline of Scott's ghost. She had recognized his green eyes, even though he had been so far away.

Now, Emily sent her thoughts toward the empty stretch of sky, calling Scott's name in her mind and asking him to appear. A light breeze caressed Emily's face, and she leaned forward, her chin tilted upward. "Is that a sign?" she whispered.

There was no answer. The air stilled once more, and Emily could hear the quiet voices of her guests drifting from the front side of the mausoleum as they asked questions of any ghosts who might be present.

"No, of course not. That was just the wind," Emily answered herself quietly.

As Emily continued to gaze west, she saw a shadow out of the corner of her eye that was darker than the other shadows around her, and it was moving. Someone was walking toward her from her left, threading their way between two tall headstones.

"Are y'all having any luck with Mayor Archer?" she asked, her eyes never leaving the horizon.

When there was no answer, Emily turned her head toward the figure.

No one was there.

Quickly, Emily scanned the area around her, but she was alone. She knew she had seen someone walking toward her. Just a dark silhouette, really, a shadow that had been striding in her direction.

There were mausoleums nearby, but the person had been too close to Emily to have dived behind one of them without her noticing.

Emily pulled her flashlight from her pocket. Even with the illumination, she didn't see anyone. She pointed the beam at the ground, tracing the path the person had been walking, but she couldn't discern any footsteps, either.

That doesn't mean anything, Emily told herself firmly. *The ground is dry, so I doubt any of us are leaving tracks.*

Still, Emily felt a strange prickling sensation on the back of her neck, and she had to admit to herself she was feeling a little nervous. She turned and walked quickly to the front of the mausoleum, calling, "It's just me! I'm not a ghost!" She didn't want her guests to hear the crunch of grass and think they were hearing phantom footsteps.

All six of the ghost hunters were seated on the ground in a semi-circle, facing the front of the mausoleum. They looked up at Emily, who stood there awkwardly. She cleared her throat, looked away, and shifted from one foot to the other, suddenly feeling self-conscious.

"Uh, did one of you just walk over to where I've been standing?" she asked, looking at them sheepishly.

Six heads shook back and forth.

"That's what I thought. It seems someone has shown up to have a chat with y'all, but they came by my side of the mausoleum instead."

There was a collective gasp, and Emily relaxed. She wasn't used to being the one to report paranormal activity to ghost hunters, and there was some part of her that had worried they would think she was making it up. She had heard too many stories about allegedly haunted places getting caught in the act of faking it all for publicity.

Emily related what she had seen, and Marlon quickly chose three members to take equipment to that spot. "Emily, please show them exactly where you were and where you saw the shadow figure. The rest of us will stay here on this side, and we'll all keep our eyes peeled!"

After doing as Marlon had requested, Emily retreated only two steps back from the three guests who were now taking photos and video of the area she had been standing in when she saw the mysterious form. She didn't want to wander off by herself again.

It wasn't until someone asked, "Do you have a message for us?" that Emily suddenly thought of Scott. She had been looking for his ghost off in the distance, but had it been him walking toward her?

No, she told herself. This figure had been shorter than Scott. Also, Emily felt like she would have instinctively known if it had been her late husband coming to say hello.

Charlie, one of the guests who had accompanied Emily, gave a shout nearly forty minutes later. It had been quiet up until then, and even Emily was beginning to feel bored. Charlie sounded more surprised than scared, but nevertheless, Emily and the other two ghost hunters stationed behind the mausoleum started.

Charlie was pointing toward an oak tree. "It was just there! I saw it!"

"What did it look like?" one of the ghost hunters asked at the same time the other said, "What was it doing?"

"It looked like a man walking toward us," Charlie answered, his voice shaking slightly. He looked excited, and

Emily knew the quaver in his voice was from adrenaline coursing through him. "I saw him out of the corner of my eye, and he ducked behind the tree." Charlie started moving toward it, slowing as he neared the thick trunk. He tiptoed closer, then leaned forward to peek behind the oak. As he returned, Emily could see the way his shoulders slumped. "No one's there."

While Charlie and the other guests felt disappointed, Emily simply felt perplexed. She wanted to know if this was the same ghost who was making the loud banging sounds or someone else. Her list of questions about paranormal activity in Hilltop Cemetery seemed to be getting longer, and she wondered how many ghost-hunting teams would visit before she began getting some answers.

Finally, at one o'clock in the morning, Marlon called it a night. By that time, the ghost hunters were yawning, and Emily felt slightly chilled. She figured everyone was as anxious as she was for a warm, soft bed.

Emily led the way back to the house, and as soon as she put her foot on the first porch step, a loud bang echoed from the direction of the cemetery. As her guests grumbled about the bad timing, Emily wondered if it was, in fact, designed to taunt them. Now that they were leaving, whatever ghost responsible for the sound was clanging away.

It's like the ghost is sticking his tongue out at us and shouting, "You can't catch me!"

Too tired to really care, Emily ushered her guests inside, locked the door, and wished them all a good night. They requested breakfast at nine o'clock again, and Emily readily approved of the plan. She was in bed just ten minutes later.

The next morning, Emily was putting breakfast on the sideboard in the dining room when she heard the sound of a key in the front door lock. A moment later, the door creaked open slowly, but there was no sound of footsteps on the wooden hallway floor.

Curious about the silence, Emily walked to the dining room door and looked down the hallway. She saw Clint standing at the threshold, the key still gripped tightly in one hand. He was staring straight ahead, down the length of the hall, but Emily sensed he wasn't really seeing the scene before him. He had a slightly dazed look, and his face was pale.

"Clint?" Emily asked gently. "Did you see a ghost?" She followed Clint's gaze but saw nothing out of the ordinary.

Clint shook his head almost imperceptibly.

Emily took a few steps toward him, walking carefully as if worried she might startle him. "What's wrong? Are you not feeling well?"

Clint blinked, and his face crumpled. The house key fell to the floor as he clamped his hands together, and Emily had the fleeting thought that he looked like he was praying or pleading for mercy. Clint's head bent, but he raised his eyes to look at Emily. "It's my mom," he said, his voice choked with restrained emotion. "They think she killed that man."

6

For a moment, Emily was too shocked to say or do anything. She simply stood there, staring at Clint wordlessly. It was a loud sniff from Clint that finally spurred Emily into action, and she quickly stepped forward and pulled him into a hug. Clint buried his face in Emily's shoulder, and she heard a muffled sob as his body shook.

What do I even say? Someone has accused his own mother of murder!

Emily tried to imagine Trish in handcuffs. She was not a woman Emily pictured going to jail quietly. "Where is your mom now?" she asked gently.

Clint took a couple of deep breaths, and his voice was muffled as he spoke into Emily's shoulder. "At home. The police brought her in for questioning last night, and they said she could go home, but she's not allowed to leave town."

"So, she hasn't been arrested? The police haven't actually charged her with…" Emily trailed off before the word "murder" came out of her mouth.

"No, not yet." Clint straightened up as footsteps sounded on the stairs, first going down, then heading back up.

"Why do they suspect your mom? Did she even know

Thornton Daley?" Emily kept her voice low so whomever had been on the stairs wouldn't overhear.

"He died after eating her biscuits. They had ground-up peanuts in them, and he went into, into…"

"Anaphylaxis," Emily supplied. "But your mom doesn't use peanuts in anything she sells at the bakery, does she?"

"No."

"That means Thornton was allergic to peanuts, and someone knew it."

Clint nodded. "She thinks somebody bought her biscuits, then put the ground-up peanuts in them. The police asked Mom a lot of questions about the customers she had the day before they found the body in the cemetery."

Emily squeezed Clint's shoulder reassuringly. "That's good news for your mom. They probably realize she's not likely to have done it herself. And if the police search her bakery and don't find any peanuts, that will be even better."

"That's what she told me, too. They're searching the bakery today, so she's at home, waiting to find out what happens."

"Why don't you go back home? I'm sure you'd much rather be with your mom right now, and I know she would appreciate having the moral support."

"No." Clint shook his head firmly. "Since the police are at the bakery, it's closed today, and who knows when Mom will be able to reopen? I'd rather be working and making some money for my family than sitting at home."

Emily smiled at Clint's desire to help not just his mom but his whole family. He didn't earn a lot working for Emily—he only came in two days a week, and she couldn't afford to pay him much—but she knew that, right then, he would feel like every penny counted. "All right," she told him. "Since you're staying here, that frees me up to go see your mom. You sit here and earn money, and I'll provide Trish with the moral support."

Before leaving for the Alden house, Emily went upstairs, where she found her guests huddled together on the landing. They didn't seem like they had been trying to eavesdrop. Rather, they seemed to be waiting for some cue that it was okay to come downstairs. Quietly, Emily told them Clint's mom had been taken in for questioning in a murder investigation. She skipped the part about Trish being a suspect, as well as the part about the biscuits being used in the murder. Trish's biscuits were among the baked goods downstairs in the dining room, waiting for Emily's guests, and there was no reason to make anyone lose their appetite. Emily got confused looks when she tried to ask casually, "Do any of you have a peanut allergy?" Fortunately, everyone said no. Emily doubted there were peanuts in any of the biscuits Trish had delivered to her, but it seemed better to be safe than sorry.

By the time Emily left the house, the color had come back into Clint's cheeks, and he was busy checking online reservation requests. The distraction, Emily decided, might be better for him than her suggestion that he go back home. Her guests were all in the dining room, though they seemed subdued in light of Emily's news.

As Emily drove to Trish's house, she realized Clint wasn't the only one who was reeling from the news. She had been so absorbed in comforting Clint—and so shocked at the idea anyone could suspect Trish of murder—that she hadn't had a chance to process her own feelings about it. Emily had been so hopeful about staying out of Thornton's murder investigation, ready to let at least one murder case in Oak Hill run its course without feeling the need to get involved. And yet, despite her determination, the murder case had come crashing into her life with the news one of her friends was so closely tied to it. Even if Trish was innocent, which Emily was absolutely convinced of, she was still intrinsically tied to Thornton Daley's murder, thanks to her biscuits.

Trish and her husband, Wayne, had bought a former cattle ranch after Clint had been born. The house wasn't much bigger than the ones in town, but Clint and his little sister, Tanya, got to grow up with a lot of land to run around on. Trish had once told Emily she suspected her kids would live in the old barn if she would let them, because they couldn't get enough of the musty old hayloft.

As Emily pulled into the long driveway that led to the house, she steeled herself for the awkward conversation that was coming. She wasn't sure how to start, though she knew Trish was the type who would appreciate a direct approach.

Emily, as it turned out, shouldn't have worried about it, since it was Trish who dove right in. When she answered the door, she looked more put-together than Emily had expected. Trish had done her makeup, and she was wearing a nice blouse with her dark-blue jeans. "I got dressed up so if they come to arrest me, I don't go to jail looking like a slob," Trish said in greeting, gesturing to herself. "I'm always the one with the latest town gossip, Emily, and now I *am* the town gossip. Come on in."

Emily followed Trish to the living room, then sat down while Trish went to the kitchen to pour two cups of coffee. When she came back, she had put the coffee cups plus a few scones onto a tray. Trish put the tray on the coffee table while saying, "If you're brave enough, I thought you might like these raisin cinnamon scones. I promise they won't kill you. Frankly, I think the only reason I haven't been arrested yet is that half the police department buys coffee and a bagel from me every day. They'd rather have me baking for them than sitting in a jail cell."

"I don't know how you can have a sense of humor

about all this," Emily said, leaning forward from her spot on the couch and gladly taking a scone.

Trish shrugged. "What else can I do? It won't help to sit here and worry. I didn't kill Thornton, and it will all get sorted out eventually."

"It will," Emily said reassuringly.

"Honestly, I'm more worried about what this will do to my bakery. Even though I fully expect the police to find the real murderer, my name is going to get dragged through the mud first, and I'm concerned people won't want to do business with me anymore." Trish flopped back against the couch cushions, and for the first time since arriving, Emily saw the concern hiding under Trish's efforts to make light of the situation.

"How did the police know it was your biscuits that killed Thornton, anyway? Did they do a taste test?"

"My biscuits are pretty well-known around town, and there aren't that many of us making them. The size, the shape, the flakiness: the police said they recognized my work right away, even though the biscuit was stuffed into Thornton's mouth." Trish paused and made a gagging noise. "They didn't tell me how many he actually ate, but it was obviously enough to be lethal."

"Clint confirmed what I already knew: you don't use peanuts in any of your baked goods. That right there should check you off the police's list."

"I could have brought in only what I needed to lace that batch of biscuits," Trish said. "The police were kind enough to point that out. Plus…" Trish trailed off, and she frowned.

"Plus, what?" Emily leaned forward and looked at her friend sympathetically. "It's okay. You can tell me."

"Well, you know how Thornton never said a kind word about anybody's food? He bashed my biscuits a few years ago, and I made a big fuss about it. I don't know if you remember, but I even took out an ad in the paper that said I'd give a full refund to anyone who bought a biscuit and didn't like it. I got a ton of business from that, and a lot of local cafe and restaurant owners came in just to give me a high-five for not taking Thornton's nastiness lying down. At the time, I thought I was being clever. Now, though, I wonder if the police are going to use it against me."

Emily laughed incredulously. "If they're going to consider that as a motive, then they're going to have a long list of suspects. Remember when Thornton reviewed Morelli's and called it the worst spaghetti he'd ever had? They bragged about that on their sign board out front for weeks! At some point, getting a terrible review from Thornton Daley became a badge of honor for Oak Hill's restaurants."

Trish leaned forward and picked up her coffee cup. "You're right. You make me feel better, Emily. You've been caught up in more than your share of murder investigations lately, so if you don't feel like I should be panicking, then neither do I."

"Maybe I can be a character witness. I can testify that you've never poisoned any of my guests!" Emily said, then turned serious again. "I think it will all work out, Trish. And I know you're worried about losing business, but we're talking about Oak Hill here. For every person who will want to steer clear of you, there will be five more who go to Grainy Day *because* of this scandal."

"That's a good point. People will want to try out the murder biscuits for themselves."

Emily snickered. "Once we're past all this, I dare you to actually call them that on your menu board."

"It's got a nice ring to it," Trish agreed, smiling. "Instead of my Basket Full of Biscuits special, I can offer a Murder Biscuit Challenge. Either you eat them and live, or your ghost gets to haunt my bakery!"

Emily took a bite of scone and chewed thoughtfully for a few moments. "Maybe that's already happening," she said slowly.

Trish sat up straight, her coffee nearly sloshing over the rim of the cup. "Oh! All of my appliances getting unplugged! You think it's the ghost of Thornton Daley?"

"Maybe. Think about it: you yourself said it felt like something was trying to prevent you from doing your job. Maybe Thornton doesn't want you baking more biscuits!"

"It started Tuesday night, when my fridge got unplugged. That was the day his body was found," Trish noted.

"I had assumed your new haunting was part of"— Emily waved both hands in circles—"whatever is causing all of these Oak Hill ghosts to act up, but maybe your haunting is about the murder, instead."

"I assume I need to give Sage a call?" Trish asked.

"I think it's a good idea. Would you be okay with us conducting a séance in your bakery?"

Trish grinned. "Of course. I have nothing to hide!"

Emily volunteered to call Sage, though it went straight to voicemail. She left a message, explaining she and Trish were hoping to find out if it was, in fact, the ghost of Thornton Daley haunting Grainy Day Bakery. Just a few minutes after Emily hung up, Trish's phone rang. Trish said very little during the short call, and after she hung up, her expression was a strange mixture of relief, confusion, and anger.

Trish took a deep breath and blew it out in a rush. "The police are finished searching my bakery," she said in a flat tone. "They said all of my appliances were unplugged, which means neither my fridge nor my freezer were the correct temperature. I'm going to have to throw out every single thing I had in them! That's so much money lost!"

Emily frowned. "Can't your insurance cover it?"

"I don't think my policy covers ghosts." Trish picked up a scone and bit into it aggressively.

"Did the police say anything else?"

"The detective said they swabbed surfaces to look for traces of peanuts, but again, I don't use them, so I'm not overly worried."

"Was that Detective Hernandez on the phone, then?"

Emily knew there was no point putting in a good word with him about Trish: Danny was too by-the-book to simply dismiss Trish as a suspect because Emily said she was too sweet to kill someone. Emily did, however, wonder if it would be worth telling him the ghost of Thornton Daley might be haunting the bakery. Danny was a firm believer in the paranormal, and he would take anything they gleaned from a séance seriously.

"Yeah, the cute guy that has all the single ladies of Oak Hill wound up," Trish said, then added, "and some of the single guys, for that matter."

"He's used information from Sage's spirit communication before. If we get anywhere with your ghost, it might be helpful in further proving your innocence."

"Let's hope it doesn't come to that."

Emily left shortly after, since she needed to get back to Eternal Rest to neaten the guest rooms and take care of some other chores. Trish's phone had rung every few minutes with friends and family calling to check in on her as word about her biscuits spread through Oak Hill, so Emily knew she wouldn't be feeling lonely.

As soon as she was back home, Emily checked on Clint. He was on the phone, and his tone seemed perkier. It appeared the distraction of work really was helping his spirits recover.

Emily was halfway through making the bed in the fourth and final room when Sage called her back. "Count me in, but it's going to have to be early," Sage said after Emily had given her more details.

"Do you have dinner plans with Jen?"

"No, I'm just too tired to stay up late. In fact, I'd like to do this as soon as I've seen my last client for the day. Can Trish let us in at five thirty?"

Emily promised to check with Trish, then hung up feeling worried about her best friend. Emily had seen Sage get drained of energy by a dark entity the two of them had encountered while searching for Scott's ghost, and she couldn't help but wonder if this lingering exhaustion was somehow related.

When Emily proposed an afternoon séance to Trish, she applauded how quickly Emily and Sage wanted to get some answers but said she didn't feel up to going into town. "I'm just not ready to run into anyone, you know?" Trish said. "You and Sage go, though. Clint has a key he can loan you."

Emily assured her she understood Trish's reluctance to leave the house and promised to fill her in on anything that happened. When she relayed the plan to Clint, she asked him if he minded staying a little late so someone was at the house until she got home from the bakery. Clint readily agreed as he slid his bakery key off his key ring and handed it to Emily. She knew he was grateful for the extra money, so it was an ideal setup for the both of them.

Trish had instructed Sage and Emily to go in the back door, saying there would be too many prying eyes around the downtown square if they just waltzed in through the front door. At twenty minutes after five, Emily pulled onto the street along the square where Grainy Day was located, but she kept driving to the end of the row of buildings. She drove around to the alley that ran behind them, and as she parked, she noticed Sage was already waiting for her.

As Emily got out of her car, she was concerned to see dark circles under Sage's eyes. Even Sage's hair seemed less spiked than usual, as if it were too tired to stick straight up. Emily gave Sage a quick hug. "Thanks for doing this," she said earnestly.

"Of course. You think I want Trish going to jail? I can't live without her croissants! Now, let's get to it, so I can go home, eat dinner, and fall into bed!"

Emily unlocked the door and soon found herself inside

the kitchen. She punched in the code for the security system, grateful Trish had thought to pass it along, then turned on the lights. However thorough the search that morning might have been, it appeared the police had at least put things back where they belonged. Even the fridge, Emily noticed, had been plugged back in. She dropped her purse on a stainless steel work surface and said, "Where do you want to do this?"

Sage walked slowly through the kitchen, then out into the customer area before returning to stand by Emily. She put one hand against her chest. "There's a concentration of energy back here, close to the oven. I sense anger. I can feel it like a pressure against my ribcage. Let's sit on the floor over there."

As Emily settled in, Sage quickly produced her usual séance tools: a purple seven-day candle, a bell, paper, a pencil, and a silver dollar. She sat down and lit the candle, then groaned. "Em, would you please get the lights?"

Emily complied, though the interior of the bakery was hardly dark, even with the lights turned off. Late-afternoon daylight still streamed through the large front windows, and the customer area was separated from the kitchen only by the counter and display cases, so the kitchen area was merely dim. As Emily sat down again, she noticed the way the hum of the fridge abruptly ceased. Quickly, she jumped to her feet and hurried to the fridge. She laughed self-consciously as she told Sage, "It just cycled off. I thought maybe it had been unplugged!"

For the third time, Emily sat down. Sage wasted no time in beginning to try establishing contact with Grainy Day's new ghost. Her voice was lower and more monotone as she said, "We know there is a spirit here with us. What we want to know is who you are, and why you are haunting this place."

After a few moments of silence, Sage said in her normal voice, "I still sense the anger but also fear. I think whatever is here might be a little afraid of us."

"We're here to help you," Emily said, addressing the area of the oven. She slowed her breathing down, trying to relax and focus on the present moment.

Suddenly, Emily's heart seemed to lurch, and she felt her adrenaline spike as her brain told her she was in danger. She gasped. "Sage, is it a violent ghost? I feel like something bad is going to happen. It's like I'm being threatened." Emily's head swung wildly as she looked around the kitchen, wondering where the attack would come from.

"You're not being threatened," Sage said calmly. "It's the ghost who feels that way. You're feeling its emotions. Oh, Em, that's a big step forward for you!"

"Um, thank you?" Emily squeaked out the words, still feeling too frightened to appreciate the progress she was making with her mediumship skills.

"We know you're scared," Sage said, her voice dropping as she addressed the ghost again. "Are you afraid of us, or are you showing us how you felt before you were killed?" After a long pause, Sage continued, "Maybe you're not ready to channel messages to me yet, or you don't know how. That's fine. See these items on the floor? You can blow out the candle, or ring the bell, or move the silver dollar. If you're afraid of us, can you please try to do one of those things to confirm it?"

Emily stared at the items Sage had mentioned, and the candle flickered briefly. She wasn't sure if it was just an air current or if the ghost was really trying to extinguish it, but Sage said encouragingly, "That's good. I'll take that to mean you're afraid of us. I assure you, Emily and I are here to help you. My name is Sage, and I'm a psychic medium. That means you and I can communicate. Do you understand?"

This time, there was a definite flicker, and the shadows danced against the walls.

Sage had a little smile on her face as she said, "If you're Thornton Daley, please do that again."

After a brief moment, the candle flickered again, then went out.

Emily whispered a quiet "wow" as Sage said, "Excellent! It's nice to meet you, Thornton. Now, let's get you the justice you deserve!" She relit the candle and said, "Blow out the candle again if you know who murdered you."

The candle extinguished immediately.

Sage relit the candle yet again, then looked at Emily. "What do you think? Should we start going through a list of suspects? It would be nice if Thornton could channel the name of his killer through me, but I don't think he's figured out how to do that yet."

Emily shrugged. "Where would we even begin? Should we just start naming every restaurant Thornton has given a bad review to over the years?"

"That could take ages. Maybe we could narrow it down by the type of food. We can ask him if he was killed by the owner of an Italian restaurant, a Mexican place, a diner, and so forth."

"That's a good idea. We might have to go read old newspapers and make a list of all the potential suspects, unless the police have done that already and can just share their list with us." As she spoke, Emily noticed a faint smell. She sniffed the air.

"I smell it, too." Sage tilted her head up and gave a big sniff. "Thornton, are you sending us a message?"

The smell increased, and soon Emily recognized the scent of butter and flour. "I think it's fresh-baked biscuits!"

Sage sighed. "Yes, Thornton, we know you were killed by biscuits that had peanuts in them."

The smell got stronger in response. "Are you trying to say Trish Alden, who owns this bakery, killed you?"

The candle snuffed out.

Emily could see Sage shaking her head slowly as she said, "You're wrong. Trish did not kill you. Someone took her biscuits and added the ground-up peanuts. Trish doesn't even have peanuts in this bakery."

The bell began to tinkle. Emily looked at it, and in the dim light from outside, she could see it was still sitting in its place on the floor. Somehow, Thornton's ghost was moving the clapper inside it.

The monotone voice Sage used when speaking to ghosts disappeared, and now she spoke to Thornton as if he were a stubborn child. "No, Thornton. Someone murdered you, but it was not Trish. I need you to think about who would have had a good reason to kill you."

The smell of biscuits faded, and Sage relit the candle, but the flame held steady. Sage drummed her fingers impatiently against the floor. "He seems fixed on Trish. I'm betting he has no idea who killed him, and he's making the assumption it was Trish since it was her biscuits that did him in."

"So much for my hope that we'd learn something the police could use," Emily said. "We can't exactly go to Danny and tell him the ghost is accusing Trish."

"We could, but we know that's not true." Sage paused, then said thoughtfully, "Actually, it could be true. It's entirely possible Trish killed Thornton."

"Sage!" Emily cried, appalled.

"She could have! I don't think she did, of course, but I'm saying it's possible. She didn't like him, and she would obviously have had access to her own biscuits."

"And then what? Tiny little Trish picked up a dead

man, hauled him to Memorial Garden Cemetery, and dug his grave herself?"

Before Sage could respond, loud popping sounds came from every direction. Emily turned quickly, just as something small and hard struck her face.

"Ow!" Emily cried, her hand reaching up to her stinging cheek. The popping noises were followed by multiple thumps all around the kitchen. Sage was already getting to her feet, and a few seconds later, the overhead lights came on.

Emily glanced down to her left, the side the object that hit her had come from, and saw a power cord lying next to her. The metal prongs must have been what struck her cheek. Slowly, she rose and began to survey the kitchen. Every single power cord had been ripped out of its socket. The plug for the fridge had been yanked so violently the plastic outlet cover had cracked, one piece now lying on the floor.

"Thornton really, really thinks Trish did it," Sage said calmly.

The lights overhead flickered a few times, and Sage looked up at them, her eyes narrowed. "Yes, Thornton, we got the message. Still, I want you to think of other people who might have wanted to kill you. Please. We'll come back some other time, when you've had a chance to work on your list of suspects!"

"Thank you for talking to us!" Emily called, at least trying to end the séance on a friendly note. If Thornton's ghost was behaving so badly at the mere mention of Trish, then Emily hated to think what would happen when she came to reopen the bakery.

Emily and Sage plugged in all the appliances before locking up the bakery, despite their expectation Thornton would simply pull them right back out again. As they walked together into the alley, Sage said, "I've been thinking about what you said, Em. Detective Hernandez takes the information we learn from ghosts seriously, and this would look bad for Trish if he finds out how certain Thornton is that she killed him. When you call Trish to fill her in on what happened today, can you ask her to keep quiet about our séance?"

"I was already planning to," Emily agreed.

When they reached Emily's car, Sage gave Emily a hug. "I'm proud of you!" she said. "It's exciting to see you making progress."

Emily thanked Sage, who wished her a good night and continued walking, heading to her car that was still parked at her office building a couple blocks away. Sage had waved off Emily's offer of a ride, saying the exercise might perk her up a little.

As Emily turned onto the street that ran along the square, she noticed a man pulling on the front door of Grainy Day Bakery. He was tall and slender, which made his white cowboy hat look comically large.

Emily dove into a parking spot in front of the bakery and lowered her window. "She's closed today," she called helpfully.

The man turned, a disappointed expression on his tanned, deeply lined face. "Guess I'll have to wait until tomorrow," he said.

"I don't think the bakery will be open tomorrow, either," Emily said. "Saturday is probably a better bet." Emily realized the man wasn't the only one caught off-guard: she had been so focused on helping Trish, she hadn't even thought about how the bakery's closure affected her. She made a mental note to stop at the grocery store on the way home to get breakfast food for the next two mornings.

The man nodded grimly as he sauntered toward Emily's car. "Guess I'll just have to be patient, then. I'm opening up a barbecue restaurant next month, and I was hoping to talk to Trish about serving her biscuits there."

"Oh!" Emily hesitated, feeling awkward. "Well, ah, I don't know if you've heard the news, but, um—"

The man's laughter broke into Emily's halting words. "Oh, I know all about her biscuit drama! I was already hoping to serve Trish's biscuits at my place, since I doubt I could make my own any better than hers, but now I'm even more excited by the idea! Oak Hill loves a good scandal, and who won't want to dare their friends and family to try the biscuit that comes with their pulled pork plate?"

Emily smiled as politely as she could, slightly horrified by the idea. It had been one thing for Trish to joke about it, but here was a complete stranger trying to capitalize on the murder. Then again, Emily thought, maybe Trish was onto something with her Murder Biscuit Challenge idea.

Seeming to sense Emily was feeling uncomfortable, the man stepped forward, his hand extended. "Sorry, sometimes my business drive oversteps my manners. I'm Allen Gerson. Is Trish a friend of yours?"

"Emily Buchanan," Emily answered, shaking his hand through her open car window. "Yeah, I've known Trish for years. I serve her baked goods at my bed and breakfast."

Allen laughed, the skin around his faded blue eyes crinkling. "Maybe you'll get some extra business because of those risky biscuits, too!"

Emily opened her mouth to explain she was already getting extra business because of other murders, but instead, she simply smiled and said, "Maybe. Good luck with your new restaurant, Allen. I had heard a rumor we were getting a barbecue place here in town, and I look forward to trying it out."

Allen reached into his shirt pocket, pulled out a business card, and handed it to Emily with a flourish. "When you come, this will get you a discount." He winked. "Have a good night, Emily. Nice to meet you." With that, he turned and walked a few parking places away, where he climbed into a big pick-up truck.

Emily shook her head as she backed out of the parking space, wondering if she should even tell Trish about the encounter. She wanted to forewarn her friend that she wasn't the only one who had already thought of the marketing value of murder biscuits. Of course, for Trish it had been something to laugh at. For Allen Gerson, it was a serious business proposal.

Clint looked eager for news about the séance when Emily got back home, but she only gave him the barest of details. Instead, she promised to call Trish and tell her everything the second Clint headed out for the day, saying his mother could decide what to share with him.

Emily couldn't remember ever feeling so reluctant to make a phone call, and she sat stiffly on the sofa, staring out the front windows as she talked. She hated telling Trish they had been successful in confirming it was the ghost of Thornton Daley haunting her bakery, but that he was absolutely convinced she was his killer. Trish was understandably disappointed when Emily finished her story, and she was even a little angry Thornton was being so stubborn. When Emily warned her she would probably experience some paranormal activity when she reopened the bakery, Trish brushed it off. She planned to take inventory of everything that needed to be replaced on Friday, and she said Clint would be with her, so she didn't have to face Thornton alone.

When Emily returned to her desk, she saw Kelly had left a note on the paper next to the laptop. *Saw him this afternoon!!!*

"Thank you for letting me know, Kelly!" Emily called to the room. "Is he doing better?"

Emily turned and walked through the parlor, her back to the desk, waiting for Kelly to respond. *Just once,* Emily thought, *I'd love to see that pen moving on its own.*

When she returned to her desk, Kelly had answered, *Yes! So bright!*

Emily praised Kelly's keen eye some more and told her to keep up the good work. She was beaming as she headed to the kitchen to make dinner. While she cooked, Marlon called to say he and his team were wrapping up dinner in town, then going straight to Oak Hill High School. He still had the key to the front door, so Emily wished them luck and promised she'd want to hear all the details on Friday morning.

It was only after Emily ate, washed the dishes, and prepped the coffee maker for the next morning that she returned to the parlor and saw Kelly had added more text to the paper. This writing was a little smaller, and Emily felt nervous before she even read it. When Kelly was happy, Emily had realized, she wrote in huge, swooping letters. When she was scared or unhappy, she wrote in a smaller, more timid hand.

Saw others, too. Just passing through. Heading toward downtown.

Emily frowned. It wasn't bad news, like she had anticipated, but it was odd. She had only rarely heard about ghosts that were able to travel from one place to another, like Scott. Emily felt a stab of jealousy that these ghosts were obviously strong enough to pass through the psychic barrier that surrounded Oak Hill, while Scott was trapped outside of it.

"Good to know, Kelly," Emily said. "Can you and Mrs. Thompson please keep an eye out for any more strange activity?"

There was a loud knock on the wall above Emily's desk as the ghost of Mrs. Thompson, Emily's former assistant, confirmed the ghosts of Eternal Rest would be on the lookout.

"Thanks. Good night, ladies."

On Friday morning, Emily got up earlier than her alarm. Between Thornton Daley's ghost haunting Grainy Day Bakery, Trish being a murder suspect, and the news that other ghosts were traveling to Oak Hill, Emily's brain snapped out of sleep and started racing at full speed before the sun was above the horizon. Figuring there was no point in trying to fall back to sleep, Emily got up, showered, and started her day.

It was too early to prep breakfast for her guests, so Emily started in on quiet tasks. She checked her emails, paid a few bills, and dusted the parlor and dining room. She got breakfast ready at half past eight, when she started hearing signs of life from her guests upstairs. Once Emily had the trays arranged in the dining room, she went onto the front porch to water a few potted plants.

Emily turned left at the bottom of the front porch steps so she could fill the watering can at the spigot on the side of the house. As she walked, she glanced at Hilltop Cemetery. The green leaves of the oak trees seemed to shimmer in the morning sun. Emily's eyes drifted from the treetops down to the iron gate, and she noticed two people exiting the cemetery. Instead of being dressed for walking or jogging, like most people who visited Hilltop that early in the day, these two were in matching navy-blue uniforms.

Emily looked toward the parking lot and saw a police car parked there.

Overcome by curiosity—as well as concern that something bad had happened on her property—Emily dropped her watering can in the grass and began walking quickly toward the police officers. They had nearly reached their patrol car by the time Emily was in shouting distance, and she called a loud good morning to get their attention.

Emily didn't recognize the man and woman who turned to face her, looking startled at being hailed. They both nodded grimly at her, then turned away and continued walking. They got in the car and pulled out of the parking lot before Emily could reach them. She stood there for a moment, halfway between the cemetery gate and the parking lot, out of breath and confused. She got the impression the officers didn't want to discuss their business with her, and she wondered what could possibly be happening that would make them hesitant to talk. For a brief, terrifying moment, Emily thought maybe another murder victim had been found in Hilltop.

No, she told herself. *If there was a body, they would have stayed to guard it. Maybe they're looking for someone, and they know the cemetery is a good hiding place.*

Emily stood there for a few moments, trying to think of other reasons the police might be checking out the cemetery. She even told herself it was possible one of them had an ancestor buried there, and they were simply stopping by to visit. The way they had looked at her, though, said otherwise.

"Danny can tell me," Emily said to herself, realizing there was an easy way to find out what was going on. She pulled her cell phone out of the back pocket of her black jeans and called Danny Hernandez.

"Detective Hernandez," he answered smoothly on the second ring.

"Danny, it's Emily Buchanan."

"Oh, Emily," Danny said stiffly. "How are you this morning?"

"I'm a little worried. Why were the police patrolling my cemetery just now?"

Danny was silent for a few moments, and finally he said firmly, "I can't tell you that."

"It's my property. If something is happening on my land, I'd like to know what it is."

"It's police business, Emily, and it doesn't have to do with your land."

"Then why were your officers on my land, if their business doesn't involve it?" Emily was surprised to feel a stab of anger.

"I can't tell you that," Danny repeated. He sounded almost sympathetic, and that just annoyed Emily more. She was used to him being open and honest about things, and his reluctance to tell her what might be happening at her cemetery was frustrating.

Danny sighed and continued, "Emily, they weren't… Those officers are… Look, I'm going to be straight with you. You've been caught up in several murder investigations recently, and you don't need to be involved in another one. The less you know, the better."

"This is about Thornton Daley's death, then."

When Danny remained stoically silent, Emily added, "Is Thornton's murder somehow connected with Hilltop Cemetery?"

"I can't tell you that," Danny said for the third time.

"Then what can you tell me?" Emily asked.

This time, Danny's voice was sharp with impatience. "I can tell you that you have nothing to worry about. Keep to yourself, and don't go looking into things that don't involve you."

"But if Hilltop is connected to the murder, then it does involve me, Danny. That's my property."

"You are not involved in this case." Danny enunciated every word, like he was talking to a stubborn child.

Emily could hear the growing tension in Danny's voice, and she knew continuing to push back would be pointless. "Okay," she said after a moment. "But promise me one thing, Danny: if something is happening at my cemetery that might put me or my guests in danger, I want you to tell me immediately."

"Of course I will. You know that."

"Okay. Bye." Emily hung up, feeling deflated. Her anger wasn't just because Danny refused to fill her in. It was also the tone he'd used with her that upset her. Danny had always treated Emily like an equal, like someone he could trust. This conversation, though, had made Emily feel like a child being scolded for asking too many questions about "grown-up things," as Emily's dad had always called them.

Emily felt a strange sensation in her chest. She hated being at odds with anyone, but it hurt even more when it was with a friend.

9

Emily walked slowly on her way back to the house, taking deep breaths to calm herself down. She didn't want her guests to see her so agitated. She stopped in the side yard to pick up her abandoned watering can, and by the time she went into the dining room to check on her guests, she was able to give them a smile that at least looked genuine.

"Wait 'til you hear what happened in the high school's theater!" Marlon said after wishing her a good morning.

"Tell me!" Emily said, right as her cell phone rang again. She thought briefly it might be Danny calling her back to apologize for being so curt with her, but it was Trish's name on the caller ID. "Tell me right after I take this call," she amended.

"Hey," Emily answered as she headed into the parlor for some quiet.

"Emily, you need to get down here to the bakery!" Trish shouted into the phone. "I already called Sage, too. She's on her way!"

Trish hung up before Emily could respond. Instantly worried about what might have happened, Emily rushed into the dining room, told her guests she had to take care of an emergency, and left.

When Emily arrived at the square in downtown Oak Hill, she pulled into a parking spot near the bakery, jumped out of her car, and hurried to the front door of Grainy Day. It was locked, so Emily knocked loudly.

Sage answered the door a moment later, then let Emily in before locking up again. "I think we riled him up yesterday," Sage whispered, her eyes wide. Emily followed her toward the kitchen, stopping abruptly as soon as she saw the view beyond the front counter.

The floor was covered in what looked like white sand. Every single bag of flour and sugar had been ripped open. The gutted bags sat limply on a tall wire shelving unit, their contents spilled out onto the tile floor.

Emily just gasped.

"What should I even do?" Trish asked. Emily looked over and saw her standing on a clean patch of floor, near the fridge. Clint stood behind her, looking slightly shocked. "I can't call the police and tell them a ghost did this."

"Oh, Trish, I am so sorry," Emily said. "If we had known this would happen, we never would have tried communicating with Thornton yesterday."

Trish waved a hand toward Emily. "He was already angry before you two talked to him. I expect this would have happened no matter what." Trish sighed. "I came here to inventory what I needed to replace, but it turns out I have to replace everything! Even my dry goods are ruined."

"We'll help you clean up," Sage offered. "Point us toward the mop and broom, and we'll get started while you go to the store for new things."

"I'm not leaving more things here for the ghost to ruin," Trish said, shaking her head wildly. "I'll buy what I need and take it straight home, then bring it all with me tomorrow morning."

"Good plan," Emily said. "Like Sage said, she and I can have all this cleaned up in no time. Everything will be clean and shiny when you come back."

Trish agreed, and soon she and Clint were gone. As Sage and Emily started sweeping mounds of flour and sugar into a dustpan, Sage said, "I hate this for Trish. It's bad enough she's losing money by not being open for two days, but it's going to be expensive for her to replace so much."

"And it's not like she can file an insurance claim for this," Emily agreed. "Or can she?"

Sage shrugged. "You've got me. Trish took photos already, so maybe she can get something to help with the loss."

Getting the floor cleaned up was easy. The hard part was clearing away the layer of flour that had covered just about every visible surface. Emily had to wash six mixing bowls that had been too close to the flour and sugar explosion, and Sage found herself on a step stool, wiping a fine dust of flour off the light fixtures.

At ten o'clock, Sage grimaced. "I have to go, Em. I have a client right now, so I've got to hustle on over to my shop. Sorry to leave you here with the rest of the cleanup."

Emily shrugged. "We got most of it done, so it won't take me much longer. Thanks for helping out. Here I thought Trish had called you in to help with the ghost, not to clean up a mess!"

Sage laughed grimly. "She did call because of the ghost. I stayed to clean because she's my friend, and she needs all the help she can get right now. Thornton Daley is still so angry, and I sense frustration, too. I think he's upset that he's pointing the finger at Trish, but we're not taking him seriously."

One of the half-empty flour bags tipped forward off a shelf and fell to the floor with a dull thud, a cloud of white dust puffing up around it.

"Maybe we shouldn't encourage him," Emily noted, retrieving the broom that was propped in a corner.

"Though I do want to know how he did this without setting off the security alarm."

Sage pointed at a small device mounted on the ceiling near the back of the kitchen. "The motion detector back here in the kitchen is aimed at the door to the alley, so it didn't pick up what was happening with the shelves."

"Smart ghost," Emily said flatly.

Emily followed Sage to the front door so she could lock it behind her. As the deadbolt clanged into place, Emily suddenly realized she was alone in a building with a very angry ghost. She turned and kept her back pressed against the door as she said in her most soothing voice, "Mr. Daley, my name is Emily. You and I never met, but I assure you, I want to help you. I've helped several ghosts before, and I want to help you, too. I know you're angry and frustrated, but please, save your energy for communicating with us."

Emily stopped and listened, even though she wasn't expecting to hear any kind of response. Finally, steeling herself, she returned to the kitchen. The mess wasn't any worse, so Emily hoped Thornton had gotten the message.

Twenty minutes later, as Emily was wiping away the last of the flour and sugar, she heard a thud and the sound of shattering glass behind her. Emily whirled around and saw a dark ooze creeping across the tile floor. The ghost had thrown a jar of molasses to the ground.

"Oh, come on!" Emily shouted, too angry to even attempt being polite. "I told you we're trying to help you! Do you want our help or not? Do you want to be stuck here forever as a ghost?"

Another jar, high on a shelf, began to wobble. There was a quiet tinkling noise as it rocked against the jars that surrounded it.

Emily raised a warning finger. "No! Don't you dare! If you want us to help you, then stop it, right now!"

The jar immediately stopped moving, and Emily

huffed out her breath. "Good decision, Mr. Daley. You need to be patient, and you need to be cooperative. It might take time, but we will get justice for you."

I hope, Emily added silently. She hated the thought of Thornton's ghost haunting Grainy Day Bakery for years to come. In the past, she had wanted to find a killer to help a ghost. At the moment, she was far less concerned about Thornton and more focused on getting peace and quiet for Trish.

Still grumbling, Emily set about cleaning up the newest mess. She put on a pair of thick rubber gloves that were sitting on the edge of the sink, then picked up as much of the broken glass as possible before turning to the sticky molasses.

Emily was making a last pass across the floor with the mop when a bang sounded through the bakery. She jumped and spun around, looking to see what Thornton had done this time. Instead, she saw Trish and Clint walking in the back door.

"Sorry," Trish said when she caught sight of Emily's expression. "I didn't mean to slam the door behind me like that. I'm just angry."

"So is Thornton," Emily said. "I suggest you pack up your jars of molasses and take them home with you, too. He's already thrown one of them off the shelf."

Trish opened her mouth to reply, then stopped. Emily suspected she was about to call Thornton a name or say something disparaging about his behavior, then thought better of it. Instead, she said, "I've got some big bags under the counter over there. Clint and I can load everything up. You head on out. You've done so much work already. Thank you, Emily."

"Of course. Let me know if you have any more problems."

On the drive back to Eternal Rest, Emily realized she

and Sage still didn't know where to begin with suspects, short of their ridiculous idea to read every single food review Thornton had ever written. It would take days, if not weeks, to do, and Trish couldn't afford to have her bakery under assault for that long.

Emily forgot all about Thornton's ghost when she turned into her circular driveway and saw Reed standing at her front door. His back was to her, and as she watched, he reached forward and rang the doorbell. Emily tapped her horn, waving when Reed turned at the sound. By that time, Emily was closer to the front of the house, and she could see how drawn Reed's face looked. Instead of pulling around to the carport at the back of the house, Emily stopped right in front of the porch steps and got out of her car.

"What's wrong?" She rushed up the steps as Reed strode to meet her. A sudden thought struck her. "This has to do with the police being at Hilltop this morning, doesn't it?"

Reed nodded grimly. "I'm afraid so." His voice was unusually quiet, and Emily fought the urge to tell him that whatever it was, she didn't want to know.

"What happened in the cemetery, Reed?"

"Nothing happened in the cemetery. At least, not in this one. This is about Thornton Daley's murder. The police came here, then left because they didn't find what they were looking for. Or, rather, who."

Reed sighed, his entire body seeming to shrink. "One of the guys on my team is a suspect in Thornton's death. Jimmy Stanton."

Emily pressed a hand against her heart. "What? But Jimmy's such a nice guy! Why would the police suspect him?"

Reed walked to the swing that hung in front of the parlor windows and sat down wearily. He motioned to Emily to join him as he began, "I had the same reaction when the police showed up at Memorial Garden this morning and asked him to come to the station. Ironically, we were filling in the hole where Thornton's body had been found when they arrived. They had gone to Hilltop first, but, of course, we weren't working there this morning.

"Jimmy came back about two hours later, and I've never seen him looking so shaken. The police had been talking to friends and co-workers of Thornton's, and they found out he and Jimmy had been romantic rivals for years. They were in the same class at Oak Hill High School thirty years ago, and apparently, they've been vying for the same women ever since their junior year. Recently, Thornton was dating a woman who had a few glasses of wine at Sutter's one night and started telling everyone at the bar how Thornton treated her better than Jimmy ever had. Apparently, Jimmy had taken her out a few times, but right as things were getting more serious, Thornton swooped in and stole her away from Jimmy."

"So it's the same high school drama, even though both men must be around fifty years old now." Emily rolled her eyes. "Still, how is their rivalry a motive for murder? Surely this isn't about losing a girlfriend."

"Well"—Reed hesitated—"apparently, the woman said a lot more at the bar that I'm not going to repeat in nice company. Let's just say, she shared some very intimate details that might hurt Jimmy's chances of getting a date with anyone else."

"Oh, boy."

"Yeah. To make it worse, it's clear the grave Thornton was found in was dug with the equipment we keep there at The Garden. Obviously, Jimmy knows how to operate it."

Emily sat back. "And if the two of them grew up together, it's likely Jimmy knew about Thornton's peanut allergy."

"Of course."

"You said Jimmy came back to work, so that means he wasn't arrested."

"On what evidence? It's all just speculation right now. There were no fingerprints on the digging equipment, and, to be fair, it's not complicated to use. Anyone could figure it out if they were determined. Though, I have to say, whomever dug that hole did a pretty good job of it."

"Thornton's ghost is haunting Grainy Day Bakery," Emily told Reed. "He's convinced Trish killed him."

"You can't blame him. He died after eating her biscuits, after all," Reed said.

"I know. Sage has been communicating with him, but he's been solely focused on blaming Trish for his death. Now, though, we can ask him about Jimmy."

"Jimmy doesn't strike me as a killer, Emily. I've worked with him for years." There was a slight warning tone in Reed's voice, and his implication was clear: making assumptions or unfounded accusations could too easily hurt an innocent person. It was something he had warned her about in the past.

"And I trust your judgment," Emily reassured him. "However, his name could jumpstart Thornton and get him thinking about people other than Trish. His ghost seems fixated on her."

"Not surprising. A ghost with a grudge can be stubborn." A quiet laugh escaped Reed's lips. "Maybe that's why you're so good with ghosts: you can be stubborn, too."

Emily gave Reed a playful nudge. "Gee, thanks. Hey, since you're here, want to come in for a glass of sweet tea?"

Reed agreed quickly, but before either one of them stood up from the swing, Emily felt something press against her left side. She looked down even as the sensation sank deeper, seeming to pass right through her skin. She saw nothing, but she felt the pressure move through her body, quickly passing out again on her right side. The sensation took her breath away, and she felt a chill spread through her body. Reed gasped just as Emily stopped feeling the pressure and warmth began to return to her core, and she knew he was experiencing the same thing.

Reed's head whipped to the right, following the line the strange feeling seemed to be following. Emily leaned around him and looked in the same direction, but the porch was empty.

"Reed?" Emily's voice was shaking.

"I think it was a ghost," Reed said slowly. "That's never happened to me before, but I've heard it described. It just passed right through us."

"Why? And whose ghost was it?"

Reed gave a little shrug, apparently less concerned about the incident than Emily. "Who knows? I got the feeling it was just someone passing through. I expect we were simply in its way."

"Let's go ask." Emily rose.

"I think it's already gone," Reed said, looking again in the direction the entity had been traveling.

"I mean I'm going to ask the ghosts here. Kelly mentioned just yesterday she had seen ghosts going past, heading toward town."

Emily led Reed into the house. She paused at the parlor doorway and said, "Kelly, was that another ghost passing through from outside the psychic barrier? I'll be right back to see if you have an answer for me."

Emily continued walking to the kitchen, where she poured two glasses of iced tea. As she handed one to Reed, she asked, "Did Jimmy mention if the police have any other suspects?"

"He said the police asked him if he knew anyone else Thornton was at odds with, but as we all know, that's a long list." Reed paused, then said, "They asked him about Trish, too, but he told the police he doesn't know her that well, and he certainly doesn't know about any strife she had with Thornton."

"This isn't good for either one of our friends," Emily said with a sigh.

When they reached the parlor, Reed settled into one of the wingback chairs by the front windows while Emily proceeded to her desk. Kelly had written, *Yup, another wandering ghost. So weird!!!*

Emily thanked Kelly while noting the writing was its usual size, meaning Kelly wasn't concerned about the unexpected visitor. Emily's body relaxed, and she realized she had tensed up after the odd experience on the swing. If Kelly wasn't worried, Emily decided, then neither was she.

"I don't get it," Emily said, dropping onto the sofa. "Where are all these ghosts coming from, and where are they going?"

"I'm as curious as you are," Reed said. "I'm going to call my cousin, the one who saw Scott's spirit in a dream. She might have some idea of what's going on."

Emily stared into her glass thoughtfully. "There's a lot of paranormal activity around town right now. I had thought it was old hauntings, ones that were practically dormant, getting stirred up by something, but now I'm wondering if new ghosts are moving in."

"And if they are," Reed added, "then why? What's so special about Oak Hill? Or, is this happening in other places, too?"

"Those are all things I'd like to know. The good news is, I don't have any new residents here. For the moment, I'm only worried about one ghost, and that's Thornton Daley."

Reed and Emily eventually steered the conversation away from ghosts and murder, talking about more everyday things like how often Reed and his team were having to mow the grass at Memorial Garden Cemetery since it was summer, and how the money Emily was setting aside to get the roof fixed was growing steadily. As they talked, Emily's guests returned. After spending the previous three evenings investigating other places, they were eager to do some ghost hunting at Eternal Rest that night. They had eaten a quick lunch before coming back to nap and rest during the afternoon, so they could be refreshed and alert for the investigation later. As they all headed upstairs to the guest rooms, Reed drained his glass. "That's my cue to head back to work," he said, rising. "We'll be here at Hilltop for the rest of the day. I hope your guests have a productive night!"

"Have a good afternoon, Reed. Let me know if you or your team find another wandering spirit out there."

"Of course." Reed dropped his voice, even though Emily's guests were in their rooms, where they couldn't hear the conversation. "And I'll keep you posted on anything else I learn from Jimmy. Keep him in your thoughts. This is scary for him."

"I'll keep him right there alongside Trish," Emily promised.

Shortly after Reed left, silence fell over the house. Emily knew her guests must be either sleeping or doing quiet activities, like reading. She realized she was tiptoeing down the hall as she returned the glasses to the kitchen, afraid of disturbing the quiet.

Emily went back into the parlor and shut the door, so she could return phone calls without the sound traveling upstairs. She was soon caught up with reservation requests, and still, the house was silent.

For a moment, Emily considered taking a nap herself, but she remembered the plants on the front porch had never gotten watered. She slipped outside and took care of the task, grateful that, this time, there were no surprising visitors to see when she looked toward Hilltop. She could just make out Reed and his team working on a plot near the northern stretch of the stone wall that surrounded the cemetery.

There was nothing to stop Emily from getting in a quick nap once the watering was finished. The house was still silent, and there were no more quiet tasks that needed to be done. Emily took the cordless phone with her into the bedroom, not wanting to miss any calls from people interested in booking a stay.

Emily dozed for half an hour, when the phone woke her with a start. She yawned, then answered, "Hello, Eternal Rest Bed and Breakfast."

"Is this Emily Buchanan?" a male voice asked briskly. Emily got the distinct impression of someone staring at their watch anxiously.

"Yes."

"This is Vic Oberfeld, Editor of *The Oak Hill Monitor*." Vic was still talking at a rapid-fire pace. "Last year, Thornton Daley gave your B and B a negative review because he found the breakfast part of *bed and breakfast* to be sub-par. He said the lackluster breakfasts might be fine for out-of-town tourists who didn't know any better, but locals would be best to steer clear. Would you care to comment?"

When Emily didn't respond immediately, Vic prompted, "We're on deadline for tomorrow's edition."

Emily pinched her lips together, physically trying to hold in the smart remarks her brain was suggesting. Thornton had never even visited Eternal Rest, and his unexpected review a little more than a year before had taken Emily by surprise. As far as she understood, Thornton had heard through the grapevine that Emily had started purchasing baked goods from Grainy Day Bakery, combining them with a meat and cheese plate to create a Continental breakfast for her guests. Thornton had complained that guests at a bed and breakfast expected, and even deserved, a home-cooked hot meal.

The day the review had come out, Emily had been overwhelmed with phone calls and emails from people in the community who wanted to show their support, but it had still hurt. What had made it especially difficult to bear was the fact Emily had once made those hot breakfasts Thornton felt guests should have. She would get up early every morning to fry eggs and bacon, bake fresh biscuits—admittedly not as tasty as Trish's—and cook hash browns.

And then Scott had died, and suddenly Emily was a grieving widow trying to keep a business afloat all by herself. She didn't have time for cooking a full breakfast anymore, and she had even updated the Eternal Rest website to tell guests they would be served a Continental breakfast each morning. No one had ever complained, with the exception of Thornton Daley.

The bad review, Emily knew, had made Trish just as angry, if not more so. For her, it was a double blow, since Thornton had already given Grainy Day a negative review several years before. If Emily told the police the things Trish had said about Thornton back then, it certainly wouldn't make her look more innocent in the murder investigation.

Vic cleared his throat impatiently, and Emily's thoughts returned to the present. "No comment," she said evenly.

"Come on," Vic prodded, "don't you want to say a few words about the dead? After all, you've got a whole cemetery next door, and you were present when Thornton's body was found at Memorial Garden. You must have smiled a little to know the man who gave you such a scathing review had finally met a bad end."

"No comment," Emily repeated. "My condolences for your loss, Mr. Oberfeld." Without giving Vic a chance to respond, Emily hung up the phone. She was horrified he would imply she was happy about Thornton's death. It was also astonishing to hear Vic talking about someone on his staff, someone he had worked with for years, in such a detached way. There was no sound of sorrow in Vic's voice, just the tone of a frazzled editor who needed a good hook before deadline.

"Disgusting," Emily mumbled. She hastily grabbed her cell phone from the nightstand, where it had been sitting next to the cordless phone, and texted Trish, *If the editor of The Monitor calls you, don't bother to answer. He's just looking for drama.*

Emily went to bed Friday night feeling strangely out of sorts. Her day had started with the police showing up at Hilltop and Danny's dismissive tone with her, and it had ended with the editor of the town newspaper implying she was happy about a murder.

The one positive Emily had from the day was the way her ghosts had responded to her guests. After having a restful afternoon, the ghost hunters had started setting up their paranormal investigation equipment around five o'clock. When everything was ready to go, they went into Oak Hill for dinner, then came back to start their investigation of Eternal Rest. Within the first ten minutes, Mrs. Thompson was happily communicating with them in the dining room, knocking on the walls enthusiastically in answer to their questions. Later, someone turned toward the sideboard and saw that writing had suddenly appeared on a blank sheet of paper there: Kelly had written a short welcoming note for the group.

It was two o'clock in the morning by the time Emily went to bed, and it was three before she finally calmed her mind enough to drift into sleep.

The next morning, it wasn't Emily's alarm that woke her up, but the ringing of her cell phone. A glance at the clock showed it was only seven fifteen, and Emily was instantly worried someone was calling about an emergency. She couldn't imagine another reason someone would call so early on a Saturday. When she saw her mother's name on the caller ID, Emily's worry only increased. She answered the call as she sat up in bed, saying, "Mom, what's wrong?"

"Have you seen the newspaper?" Rayna asked in an angry tone.

Emily relaxed and flopped back against her pillows, relieved there was nothing to worry about. "I assume my name was mentioned in an article about Thornton Daley?"

"Have you not seen it?"

"No. I was still asleep. My guests did an investigation here last night."

"Oh, sorry. Well, now that you're up, you should get your copy off the front porch and take a look. It's not good, honey."

"I declined to comment, so how bad could it possibly be?"

Rayna sighed softly. "The editor wrote it as an opinion piece, and it's all about people who had reason to want Mr. Daley dead. He talks about the bad reviews he gave both you and your friend Trish, and he suggests that, of everyone in this town who disliked Mr. Daley, you had the strongest motive for murder."

Emily sat up again. "That's crazy! He gave everyone a bad review, so how am I a more likely suspect?"

"Mr. Oberfeld points out that you serve Grainy Day baked goods, and you get a lot of business because of ghosts. He, well, he implies in the article that you might get more business if there was another juicy ghost story and guests could eat the very biscuits that turned the man into a ghost to begin with. He says murdering Mr. Daley might have been a smart marketing move on your part."

Emily dropped her forehead into her free hand. "Why is everyone so fixated on these murder biscuits?" she mused, more to herself than to her mother.

"Of course, everyone knows you didn't kill him," Rayna said sympathetically, "but you know how this town is. I wanted to make sure that if you hadn't read the article yourself yet, then at least you'd hear about it from me. I didn't want you to be caught off-guard if someone else calls, or if you run errands in town later."

"I appreciate it," Emily said. "Thanks for the heads up, Mom."

"Go read it, but get yourself a cup of coffee first. Love you."

Emily did exactly as her mother advised, and although the article mentioned quite a few other people who were disgruntled with Thornton's bad reviews, her mother had been right: Emily was made to look like the prime suspect. The blow was slightly softened, just a little bit, by the way Vic cast everyone he wrote about in a suspicious light.

After she finished the article, Emily tossed the newspaper onto the coffee table in front of her, then thought better of it. She didn't want one of her guests to idly pick it up and read that their hostess might be a murderess. Emily got up from the sofa and took the newspaper straight to the recycling bin out back.

Emily was arranging fruit on a tray when her phone rang again. This time, it was Jen calling, indignant about the article. "Sage isn't up yet, but she's going to be every bit as mad as me when she sees it," Jen told Emily. "I'm just calling to let you know that Vic Oberfeld is a mean man, and it's not fair for him to publicly point the finger at you."

"Thanks, Jen. I appreciate the support."

No sooner had Emily hung up from that call than the phone rang again. She answered to hear Reed's incredulous voice. "First Trish and Jimmy, and now you," he said. "Emily, I'm sorry."

"It's fine, Reed. However, when my subscription for the newspaper runs out, I don't think I'm going to renew."

Someone Emily knew through the Oak Hill Hospitality Society called next, then Etta-Jane, the florist, followed by Jay from The Depot. Emily wasn't sure if he was calling to offer his sympathy so much as to pry for more details that he could gossip about with his diners.

By nine thirty, Emily had answered the phone thirteen times, and every single call had been about the newspaper article. She also had three voicemails from people who had called her cell phone while she'd been talking to someone on the cordless phone.

With a disgusted shake of her head, Emily glared at both phones and decided she'd had enough. She appreciated that people were on her side, but their anger only fueled hers. She wanted to forget about the article, not relive it every five minutes. She took her cell phone and the cordless phone, turned off the ringers on both, and shut them inside the hall closet. As much as Emily hated the thought of missing a call from someone who wanted to book a room, she needed a break.

Emily wished her guests a good morning when they came downstairs for breakfast at ten, then retreated to the parlor sofa with a book. She wasn't even willing to check her emails, afraid one of them might be a message of angry solidarity.

It was a relief when Emily's guests said they were heading to a nearby town that was hosting a locally grown food festival. They planned to stay there most of the day, exploring the town and sampling all the local food.

The farther they are from the gossip, the better.

Once her guests had headed out for the day, Emily walked to the hall closet and stood in front of the closed door. "I don't want to miss anyone calling to make a reservation," she debated with herself, "but I also don't want to talk to anyone about that stupid article." Emily put a hand on the knob, then stopped. "Mrs. Thompson? Good morning. Are you listening?"

A single, soft knock sounded from the wall just a few feet to Emily's right.

"Mrs. Thompson, somebody wrote something unkind about me in the newspaper, and while I appreciate people calling to tell me they support me, I don't really want to talk about it right now. Do you think it's okay if I let calls go to voicemail for a few hours? I hate making future guests wait to book their reservations."

The answering knock was so loud this time that a picture frame rattled against the wall.

"After all," Emily continued, "I'm booked solid for another six weeks. No one is calling to make a last-minute reservation."

Mrs. Thompson rapped on the wall again, and Emily took it as her former assistant agreeing with her logic. Emily missed being able to sit down for a heart-to-heart chat with Mrs. Thompson, whose wisdom and advice had always been a comfort, especially in the weeks after Scott's death. In her mind, Emily could picture Mrs. Thompson reaching out a bony hand to give Emily's fingers a surprisingly strong squeeze, telling her in a firm but gentle tone to take care of herself first and the house second.

Emily felt more certain of her decision to avoid the outside world since Mrs. Thompson had given her approval. She left the phones in the hall closet, retrieved her bucket of cleaning supplies from the kitchen, and headed upstairs to clean the guest rooms.

The physical activity was just what Emily needed, and she felt calmer with every room she completed. By the time she was giving the fourth and final room a quick glance to make sure everything was tidy, she wasn't even thinking about Thornton Daley or Vic Oberfeld.

With the upstairs clean, Emily decided it was time to get herself clean. She had skipped right past that step during the morning's drama. She planned to shower, eat lunch, then do a few small tasks around the house that would fill up her afternoon without being overwhelming.

Emily didn't even get to the showering part before the doorbell rang, followed by sharp knocking. Grumbling at the interruption and worried it was someone coming to talk about the editorial in person, Emily stalked down the hall and threw open the door. She muttered a surprised "Oh!" when she saw Trevor standing there, a worried look on his face and his hand raised to knock again.

"Thank goodness," he said, his hand dropping as his expression relaxed. "I was worried about you."

Emily rolled her eyes. "Are you here to tell me how angry you are, too?"

"Angry? No. What am I supposed to be angry about?" Now Trevor was frowning.

Emily's annoyance disappeared, and she laughed. It was a relief to know at least one friend wasn't riled up. "If you don't know what I'm talking about, then I don't know what you're talking about. Why on earth were you worried about me?"

"I've been trying to call you for the past two hours, and both of your phones keep going to voicemail. I tried texting, too. It's not like you, and I was afraid something was wrong."

"I'll explain why I'm avoiding people later, but rest assured, I'm fine."

"If you're acting like a recluse, then I assume you don't know what's going on at Trish's bakery?"

12

"What did the ghost do this time?" Emily asked, picturing even more destruction in the Grainy Day kitchen.

"Ghost?" Trevor cocked his head in confusion. "I meant the crowd. There was a horde of people out front when I drove by earlier this morning. The entire sidewalk was blocked."

"My guess is everyone wants to try Trish's murder biscuits. I doubt most people know her bakery is being haunted by the ghost of Thornton Daley, who thinks she killed him."

Trevor shook his head and laughed softly. "I keep forgetting I'm living in a small town again. Word didn't travel this fast when I was in Atlanta. Want to come see for yourself? We can grab lunch at The Depot afterward."

Emily glanced longingly over her shoulder. "I really need a shower."

"Then go shower. I'll wait in the parlor." When Emily still looked hesitant, Trevor added, "You opened the door like you were looking for a fight. I don't know what's going on, but I don't think you should be sitting at home by yourself."

Emily tried to give Trevor a scathing look, but she could feel the way her mouth was curving up in a smile. He was surprisingly perceptive sometimes, and she knew his suggestion was a good one. Going out for lunch meant she might have to talk to more people who wanted to gossip about the newspaper article, but at least she would be doing it face-to-face and with a friend by her side. "Give me twenty minutes," she promised.

It actually took Emily half an hour to get ready, but eventually she appeared in the parlor, wearing a fresh Eternal Rest button-down shirt and black jeans. Trevor offered to drive, and on the short trip to downtown, Emily told him about Vic Oberfeld's snide opinion piece.

"And here I am, taking you to both of Oak Hill's gossip headquarters," Trevor said, half teasingly and half sheepishly, when she finished.

"Actually, I think visiting Grainy Day is a good idea. Thornton's ghost is really mad at Trish, and he ruined most of her ingredients the other day. My morning was so crazy I totally forgot she was reopening the bakery today. I want to make sure she's doing all right."

Trevor reached the square and drove around to the side Grainy Day was on. Instead of a crowd in front of the door, there was now a line of people that went down the sidewalk and around the corner. Trevor whistled.

"Trish was worried no one would want to buy her baked goods anymore, since her biscuits were used as a murder weapon," Emily noted. "I told her people would probably be more excited than ever, but I didn't know she would be quite this popular!"

There wasn't a single available parking spot on the square, and Trevor had to drive another two blocks before finding an open space. As he and Emily walked to Grainy Day, every person they passed on the sidewalk was carrying a basket, box, or bag from the bakery.

Emily heard a few grumbles as she and Trevor skipped the line and went right inside, but they ignored them. Instead, they walked past the counter and into the kitchen.

Everything appeared to be in order, and Emily breathed a sigh of relief. At the moment, it seemed, Thornton's ghost was behaving.

"You were right, Emily! Everyone wants to eat the hot gossip!" Trish called. She was standing at the cash register, strands of hair sticking to her forehead. She looked exhausted, but she was also smiling. "Ooh, I should come up with a warm pastry called a Hot Gossip! What a great name! I just sent Clint to the store for more eggs and flour. Can you check the fridge for me?"

Emily knew Trish was referring to the cord, which was still securely plugged into the wall. "All good! You need any help?" Emily asked.

"Actually, I'm hoping your guests can help me. You and Sage made some progress with Thornton"—Emily heard some startled gasps at the name, and the buzz of conversation among the customers quickly silenced as everyone listened in—"but I'd like to see what else we can learn from his ghost. I would love it if y'all can come back, but I thought your guests might want to join in, too."

"I'll ask, but I'm pretty confident they'll say yes. Tonight is their last night, and they're at a food festival right now, so I'll propose the idea the second they get back."

Trish made change for a woman as she said, "I'll send them all home with a Basket Full of Biscuits as a thank you."

"I'll let you know what they say. Good luck!"

Someone Emily didn't know caught her arm as she and Trevor worked their way to the front door. "Trish mentioned the dead man. Is his ghost here?" the woman asked.

"Well," Emily said hesitantly, not sure if Trish wanted anyone to know about her haunting. Of course, Emily reminded herself, Trish had just talked about the ghost in front of a room full of customers. Besides, she reasoned, the news would probably only result in more business for the bakery. Her mind made up, Emily winked and said, "Yeah, Thornton's ghost is looking for his killer."

By the time Emily reached the sidewalk, she could hear the customers inside repeating the word "ghost" in shocked tones. Emily was just happy she had been in a crowd of people, and not one of them had mentioned Vic's finger-pointing opinion piece.

That changed the minute she and Trevor walked into The Depot. Jay was just coming out of the kitchen, and as soon as he saw Emily, he shouted, "Vic Oberfeld has no right! No one in this town thinks you would murder someone!"

Everyone seated in earshot turned to gape at Emily, and she felt her cheeks flush. "Hi, Jay," she said quietly. "We're going to grab a table out on the patio." Without waiting for a response, she turned and walked out, choosing a table in the far corner of the outdoor seating area. It would be a little hot sitting there, but Emily decided sunshine was better than embarrassment.

Trevor was nodding as he sat down. "I see why you stashed both phones in the closet."

"You sure you want to be seen in public with someone as scandalous as me?" Emily asked teasingly.

"This is nothing compared to my dad and brother."

Emily sobered quickly at the mention of Trevor's dad. "How are you doing? I meant to call you after the funeral, but I was there when that lady found Thornton's body, and then Trish was brought in for questioning, and then Thornton's ghost showed up at her bakery and started causing problems, and then the editor of the newspaper decided to make me look like Public Enemy Number One. It's been a busy week."

"Here I thought you just didn't care." Trevor smiled

briefly, then shrugged. "I feel sad, of course, but I made my peace with Dad a while back. I made the right decision to come take care of him when his cancer got bad, and I made the right decision to stay here even after he went to jail. He's not in pain now, and his past can't haunt him anymore."

Emily reached forward and covered Trevor's hand with hers. "I'm sorry I haven't been keeping a closer eye on you. You know I'm all too familiar with the grief of losing someone close. If you need to talk, I'm here."

"I know." Trevor leaned forward, his eyebrows raised. "You said you saw Thornton's body?"

"I didn't. Everyone else wanted to look in that hole, but not me. I stayed back."

"Smart. His funeral is today, actually. I went to visit Dad's grave this morning, and I ran into Reed. He was at Memorial Garden getting ready for the graveside service."

"At least Thornton's body will be resting in peace," Emily said. "Now we just need to identify his killer so his ghost can rest in peace, too."

Trevor's eyes lit up. "Let's go to the funeral!" He looked at his watch. "It's in two hours, so we can eat lunch, then head over there. Maybe we can learn something."

Emily looked at Trevor thoughtfully. "That's not a bad idea. If I killed someone, I'd probably go to the funeral to gloat. We can look for anyone acting suspicious."

"Or happy."

"Exactly. I guess you'll have to drive me home after we eat, so I can put on something fit for a funeral."

Emily and Trevor almost got through lunch without any more talk about the newspaper article. Jay sought them out as Emily was taking the last bite of her club sandwich, and he pulled an empty chair to their table and sat down. After ranting for a few minutes about the audacity of newspaper editors, Jay suddenly changed the subject, saying, "I hope you have some ghost hunters staying with you soon. This ghost in my kitchen keeps acting up. I'd like to get him to leave, or at least calm down."

"I've actually got ghost hunters staying with me right now, but they'll probably be investigating at Grainy Day tonight. I'll ask my next round of ghost hunters if they can help you, though." Emily made a mental note to add Jay to the growing list of business owners asking for an investigation.

"Grainy Day?" Jay tilted his head and looked at Emily curiously. "Does Trish have a new haunting, too? What kind of stuff is her ghost doing?"

"Looking for his killer. It's Thornton Daley."

Jay's eyes lit up. "Really? That's interesting." Jay mumbled a few words as he got up, wishing Emily and Trevor a hasty goodbye. Emily knew he was off to share the news, and she figured the crowd at Trish's was only going to get bigger.

Trevor drove Emily home and waited while she quickly changed into the same somber-looking black dress she had worn to the funeral on Tuesday. Emily's guests were still out, so she wrote them a brief note and taped it to the front door, telling them she would be home in the late afternoon. She was grateful Marlon still had the spare key, so she didn't have to worry about the group being locked out if they got back before she did.

Since Trevor also needed to put on a nicer outfit, he and Emily stopped by his childhood home—where he had been living since he had returned to Oak Hill to take care of his father—so he could change quickly, too. By the time they were finally on their way to the funeral, they were running the risk of being late.

The church where Thornton's funeral was being held was a massive granite structure three blocks off the downtown square. The crowd at Grainy Day seemed like nothing compared to the crowd heading through the arched doorway of the church. Emily and Trevor joined the throng.

Everyone arriving at the last minute, like Emily and Trevor, had to search for open spots here and there throughout the church since nearly every pew was full.

Thornton may not have been well liked, but he was at least well known, Emily thought as she and Trevor squeezed past a family to settle into the middle of a pew near the back of the church.

The service began just a few minutes later, and when Emily glanced behind her, she saw there were people standing at the back since there was nowhere left to sit. She only half listened to the preacher, her mind too absorbed in gazing at the people around her and wondering if any of them looked suspicious.

Most of them simply looked curious. Only a few actually appeared to be sad.

When the preacher called Vic Oberfeld to the pulpit to talk about Thornton's many years of service to the newspaper, Emily couldn't help wrinkling her nose in dislike. She figured she was far enough away that Vic wouldn't be able to see her expression, anyway.

Emily had never actually met Vic, though she knew his name since he had been editor of *The Oak Hill Monitor* for at least two decades. He was a short man with a halo of cropped brown hair surrounding a shiny bald spot. He wore wire-rim glasses that he constantly reached up to readjust, and Emily suspected it was simply a nervous habit.

After saying a few nice words about Thornton's work, Vic cleared his throat and said ominously, "Of course, we are all reeling from the news that our town has a murderer in its midst. Even here, today, as we mourn

Thornton's death, there are people who had reason to kill him."

There was a hum throughout the church as everyone began to whisper, looking furtively at the people around them.

Vic, seeming to savor the tension, continued, "It's no secret Thornton made some enemies with his honest opinions."

Emily bit her lip and clamped her hands together in her lap.

"I vow that I and *The Oak Hill Monitor* will work tirelessly to keep this community informed about the suspects, the evidence, and the truth that Thornton so deserves!"

There was some scattered applause, and Emily glanced at Trevor, who made a face of mock awe.

As the church began to quiet down again, one woman could be heard crying loudly. The noise grew to a hysterical sound, then shifted into what sounded like laughter. The woman's deep belly laughs cut off abruptly, and Emily wondered if she had clapped her hands over her mouth, or if someone had done it for her.

Vic smiled grimly as he finished his eulogy, apparently satisfied he was getting the right reaction out of his audience.

When the service concluded, Emily felt a tap on her shoulder as she stood. She turned around and saw the florist, Etta-Jane Nicks, whose eyebrows were arched dramatically.

"Was that Mercedes O'Brian laughing like that?" Etta-Jane asked in a loud whisper.

"I don't know who that is," Emily answered.

Etta-Jane seemed surprised. "I thought everyone knew about Mercedes! Thornton just about ruined her life!"

Emily stared at Etta-Jane, who gave a self-satisfied laugh. "Oh, yes," she said slowly, glancing around to make sure no one was listening. Her eyes landed on Trevor, and she hesitated.

"He's with me," Emily clarified.

"Mercedes and Thornton tried to go into business together some years ago," Etta-Jane began. "They were going to open a little cafe out by the Interstate, hoping to get lots of business from people on road trips who wanted to stop for a break. They even planned to build a huge parking lot so truckers could come eat." Etta-Jane leaned closer to Emily and Trevor. "I don't know what happened, but about six months after they started making the plans, word got around it was all off. Thornton had backed out of the deal, and Mercedes was stuck with a bunch of huge bills. Apparently, they had already rented a space next to a gas station, and they had started renovating the kitchen. I even heard Mercedes had to declare bankruptcy!"

"No wonder she's both laughing and crying at his funeral," Emily said under her breath.

"I can't imagine who else would have been making that racket." Etta-Jane nodded to her left. "There she goes, in the straw hat."

Emily turned as surreptitiously as she could and saw a

woman who looked to be in her late fifties walking slowly down the aisle, her arm linked through a man's. She was wearing a tight black dress and a wide black sunhat. Mercedes had a tissue pressed over her nose and mouth, and her heavy black eyeliner was streaked. As she passed, people were stopping to murmur to her or to pat her gently on the back.

"Were she and Thornton a couple?" Emily asked, noticing Mercedes was being treated more like a grieving widow than a former business partner.

"If they were, they never made it public," Etta-Jane said, but it was clear from her tone she suspected the two had, in fact, been romantically involved.

"Thanks for the intel," Emily said, giving Etta-Jane a smile.

"We're going to the graveside service, too, right?" Trevor whispered eagerly as he and Emily joined the crowd of people exiting the church.

"Absolutely."

The service at Memorial Garden didn't attract nearly the crowd the church had, and Emily assumed most people had satisfied their curiosity and didn't feel the need to go stand in the hot sun on a Saturday afternoon for someone they hardly knew. The smaller group of people gave Emily and Trevor a better chance to really look around them, and when Emily caught Reed's eye, she gave him a bashful wave. His expression was clearly asking why in the world she was there. Reed gazed at Emily with narrowed eyes for a long moment, then shook his head almost imperceptibly while turning his eyes upward. Emily knew he had figured out exactly why she was there.

The preacher spoke for a few minutes, said a prayer, and suddenly it was over. As Emily looked at the people who were beginning to talk to each other and relax, she saw a tall man with short, curly brown hair at the back of the group put on a big white cowboy hat. Without that signature hat, she hadn't recognized Allen Gerson, the owner of the barbecue restaurant that would be opening soon.

"Follow me," Emily whispered to Trevor, taking him gently by the arm and leading him toward Allen. When they reached him, he had just turned away from someone who was now heading toward the parked cars. "Mr. Gerson, right? I met you outside Grainy Day a few days ago."

Allen smiled widely. "Emily from the bed and breakfast! And just call me Allen. Is this your husband?" He turned toward Trevor and touched a hand to the brim of his hat, nodding politely.

"Uh, friend," Emily said hastily, dropping Trevor's arm. "I didn't realize you knew Thornton." Emily stopped herself before adding she also hadn't realized his interest in Trish's murder biscuits had such a personal connection.

"Oh, of course I knew the old grump! We first met at a culinary convention over in Birmingham. I've been around the food scene for a long time, and I know how important it is to be friendly with your local food critic."

"How funny that you two met in Alabama, even though you're both from Oak Hill!" Emily said.

Allen laughed. "Oh, no, I just moved here a few years back. I had planned to retire early up here, but when I realized this town didn't have a barbecue restaurant… Well, every Southern town needs good barbecue, don't you think?"

"It will be nice not having to drive to the next town over for some ribs. Well, take care, Allen. I'm sure I'll see you again soon."

"Y'all take it easy." Allen tipped his hat again and began to saunter toward his pickup truck. He paused to speak to Mercedes O'Brian briefly. She looked a little more composed than she had at the church, and she had clearly touched up her makeup on the drive from the church to the cemetery. The streaks of eyeliner and mascara were gone, and her lipstick was a bright shade of red.

Emily began to tell Trevor about Allen's interest in Trish's biscuits, but she cut off abruptly when Mercedes gave Allen a wave, then turned and walked right up to them.

"Hello," Mercedes said in a throaty voice, offering her hand to Trevor. "And who are you? Friends of Thornton's?"

"Well," Emily began, caught off guard. She hadn't expected anyone to put her on the spot that way.

Trevor came to the rescue, introducing himself and Emily, then saying smoothly, "Mr. Daley's body was discovered at my father's funeral on Tuesday. Such a shocking and tragic event. I thought coming to the service might provide some closure on what is possibly the longest week of my life."

Mercedes blinked. "Oh," she said with a note of surprise. "My condolences on your loss."

"And you have mine," Trevor replied.

Mercedes smiled sadly. "I can't decide if I'm sad or relieved. Thornton and I had a rocky history. Still, I never wanted to see him go out like this."

As Emily stood by silently, listening to the exchange, she saw a brief flicker of light around Mercedes. It seemed to outline her body, a rusty hue that shimmered and danced around her. Just as quickly as Emily had seen it, it was gone.

It's her aura. I just saw her aura. I wasn't even trying! Sage is going to be so proud.

Emily was grateful she had put a handkerchief in her purse. She quickly pulled it out and dabbed at her nose, trying to hide the excited smile she couldn't suppress. Once she was able to get her expression under control, she lowered the handkerchief and returned her attention to the conversation. Mercedes and Trevor were discussing how awkward funerals could be, especially when one wasn't overly fond of the deceased.

The man who had been escorting Mercedes down the aisle at the church came up to their group. His black suit looked expensive and expertly tailored, and he had carefully styled black hair above his high forehead. He didn't even look at Emily or Trevor. Instead, he looked pointedly at Mercedes. "Are you ready to go?" he asked in a crisp tone.

Mercedes smiled apologetically at Emily and Trevor. "This is my brother, Wynn. He's anxious to get me away from this circus."

Wynn glanced up, his brown eyes surveying Emily and Trevor suspiciously, but remained silent.

Mercedes cleared her throat. "It was kind of you both to come," she mumbled before taking Wynn's arm and turning away.

Once Mercedes was out of earshot, Trevor said, "It really wasn't kind of us to come, but it was insightful."

"You have no idea. I think I saw her aura! It was sort of brownish-red, but I don't know what that means. I'll ask Sage later."

"Congratulations! That's great progress. In the meantime, she stays on the suspect list, right?"

"Right."

"I think our work here is done. Thanks for indulging me today, Emily. It just felt like the right thing to do."

"Coming to the funeral was the right thing to do?" Emily asked, confused.

"I meant trying to find Thornton's killer. There's something satisfying about helping you with this work. Maybe 'satisfying' isn't the right word. It's fulfilling."

Emily smiled wryly. "So, when are you starting at the police academy?"

Before Trevor could reply, Emily heard a deep chuckle behind her. She turned to see Jay. His large frame was squeezed into a black suit, and he looked both sweaty and uncomfortable.

"Twice in one day, Emily!" Jay boomed. "I'm surprised to see you here."

"Honestly, Jay, I'm surprised to be here," Emily answered. "It was Trevor who suggested we should come."

Jay glanced over Emily's shoulder and harrumphed softly. "I wonder what he's going to think about you being here?" Jay gave a little nod, and Emily turned to find herself looking right at Vic Oberfeld, who was quickly approaching their little group.

"Jay, always good to see you," Vic said. "After the things Thornton said about The Depot, though, I didn't expect to find you among the mourners."

Jay laughed good-naturedly, giving no indication he was uncomfortable under Vic's suspicious gaze. "That was over a decade ago, Vic, and the review didn't stop you or anyone else in this town from eating at my place. For that matter, it didn't even stop Thornton. He never admitted it, but he liked my chili."

Vic turned his narrowed eyes to Emily. "You're Emily Buchanan. Did you come here to prove you didn't hold a grudge against Thornton?"

Emily tried to keep her expression neutral, but she failed. It was bad enough for Vic to cast her in a suspicious light in the newspaper, but somehow, doing it to her face was even worse. She felt anger rising in her again, and she fought to remain calm.

"Emily was nice enough to come today because I asked her to," Trevor broke in. "Thornton was found here just after my father's funeral on Tuesday. You can imagine how such a thing added to my grief." The challenge in Trevor's voice was clear, as if he were daring Vic to make accusations to someone who had just buried a parent. Emily had to repress a snicker when Vic's face fell, his eyes growing wide in something like panic.

Vic's mouth moved for a few seconds before he managed to get any words out. "You're one of the Williams boys. We've given your family plenty of coverage in our newspaper." With that, Vic turned and walked away.

Emily was too disgusted by Vic's comment to say anything for a moment, but she could hear Trevor muttering every mean name he could think of under his breath.

"He's got some nerve," Jay said quietly. "Though, I guess we knew that already, since he was crazy enough to deliver the eulogy."

Emily's anger quickly turned into curiosity. "Why wouldn't he speak? Thornton worked for him for years."

Jay nodded grimly. "They worked together, yes, but they weren't friends. They had a huge falling out years ago, right in the middle of the newsroom. The whole town knew every detail of that shouting match five minutes after it happened."

Jay laughed so heartily at Emily's surprised expression that she worried Vic might overhear and know they were talking about him. When his mirth had finally subsided, Jay said, "You should ask Thornton's ghost about it the next time you're at Grainy Day."

"What did they fight about?" Emily asked.

"Apparently, the newspaper was struggling financially at the time. Vic wanted Thornton to start writing more positive reviews, because one restaurant after another was pulling their advertisements in protest of the bad publicity they were getting from Thornton's food column. They didn't want to spend money with the same newspaper that trashed their food. Vic said he needed them to advertise if *The Monitor* was going to stay in business. Thornton didn't want to change his writing style, and of course, he won in the end. I've heard their relationship never recovered after that. Vic had to cut all kinds of corners to keep the newspaper afloat, until things started improving a year or two later."

Emily grinned at Jay. "The next time I'm trying to track down a murderer, I'm going to start by asking you for every bit of gossip you know about the victim. This is helpful information, Jay. Thank you."

Jay smiled proudly at Emily. "Happy to help. You two

have a nice afternoon. I've got to hustle back to the restaurant."

Emily and Trevor looked at each other excitedly as soon as Jay walked away. "That's another suspect for us to ask Thornton's ghost about," Emily enthused. "Vic Oberfeld is going on the list, right under Mercedes O'Brian."

"I imagine you feel some satisfaction in being able to point the finger at the man who pointed the finger at you," Trevor said.

"Maybe Vic didn't write that opinion piece just to be sensational. By making me and others look suspicious, it takes attention away from his own history with Thornton." Emily turned and saw Reed and his team beginning to collect a few folding chairs that had been placed by Thornton's open grave. She called his name softly and waved him over when he looked up.

"Are you having a productive funeral?" Reed asked with a smirk when he was close to Emily and Trevor.

"Yes, but I have a question for you. You mentioned one of the reasons Jimmy is a suspect is because he knows how to operate the digging equipment, but you also said anyone could figure it out if they really wanted to. My question is, could you use it to put the body in the ground, too? If someone had to drag Thornton to that hole and chuck him in, it would narrow down our list of suspects to only the really strong people."

"Our equipment here at the cemetery could be used to move anything big and heavy, including bodies," Reed said. "In fact, I think it's likely whomever did this wasn't familiar with the equipment. The digging was fairly well done, but it would have been slow-going for someone who was doing it for the first time. It's possible they were interrupted by an early-morning visitor or even someone on my team, which is why they never got to fill in the grave after they put Thornton in it."

"Even if they had finished up, wouldn't a fresh grave have raised suspicion?" Trevor asked.

"Of course," Reed agreed. "Another reason why it was probably done by someone unfamiliar with the way things run at a cemetery. We would have noticed, and we would have called the police. Hiding Thornton's body out here was a terrible idea."

Emily thanked Reed—both for his insight and for not breaking into sexton humor like he had at Mr. Williams's funeral—then told Trevor she was ready to go. "I'm worn out after our afternoon of looking for suspects," she said.

When Trevor dropped Emily off at Eternal Rest, she leaned over and gave him a hug as well as she could manage in the confines of the car. "Remember, I'm here if you need anything," she told him with feeling. "I might be out of sight, but you're never out of my mind."

"Thanks, Emily. Keep me posted on anything you learn about Thornton, okay?"

"I will." Emily slid out of the car, already thinking back over everything she and Trevor had seen and learned during the afternoon.

Emily had Eternal Rest all to herself for the moment, and she headed straight for her bedroom. She set her alarm to go off in an hour, not wanting to take another lengthy nap, and sprawled in bed. It had been a long day already, and it was only late afternoon. Trevor had told Mercedes this had been the longest week of his life, and Emily was beginning to feel it might be one of hers, as well.

Emily had been a light sleeper since Scott's death, so she was surprised when she woke with her alarm, feeling almost groggy from the deep sleep. She was even more surprised when she found her guests lounging in the parlor.

"Welcome back," Emily said, leaning through the

parlor doorway while trying to hide her embarrassment about sleeping instead of being available to her guests.

"We are stuffed!" Marlon said in answer.

"Are you too stuffed for more ghost hunting?" Emily asked hopefully.

However full and tired her guests might have been after their visit to the food festival, they all perked up at those words. Marlon asked Emily to explain.

Emily told them about Trish's request to have ghost hunters investigate her bakery, adding it was tied to a recent murder.

One of the women, Nancy, perked up at the mention of Thornton Daley. "Oh, we heard all about him!" she said enthusiastically. "I can't imagine what it was like when they found the body at that other cemetery."

"I can," Emily said sardonically. The comment went unnoticed by her guests.

"And his ghost is haunting a bakery! How cool!" It was Marlon's younger sister, Maggie, who was speaking, and Emily remembered she had been introduced as a rookie ghost hunter when the group had checked in. "We could help solve a murder!"

"That's what we're hoping for," Emily said. "I'll be there with you, as will my best friend, Sage. She's a psychic medium, and she's already communicated with Thornton's ghost a bit."

The group quickly gave Emily an enthusiastic yes, which meant she needed to call Trish to let her know. Emily felt dismay when she pulled her two phones out of the hall closet: she had twelve missed calls and seventeen text messages on her cell phone, and there were six voicemails on the cordless phone.

Emily called Trish, ignoring the waiting voicemails and text messages for the moment. Trish said she would run home for a quick shower and dinner first, and she promised to swing by Eternal Rest on the way to drop off baked goods for the next morning's breakfast. Emily breathed a sigh of relief at that last bit of news, happy she wouldn't have to assemble another substitute breakfast for her guests.

Emily was grateful she had taken the time for a nap since she would be up late helping out at Grainy Day. She texted Sage to let her know everyone would meet at eight o'clock, then reluctantly turned to all the texts and voicemails waiting for her. As expected, the vast majority of them were people calling to talk about Vic's editorial, and Emily only had to return three phone calls from people who wanted to book a stay at Eternal Rest.

Emily had just hung up the phone after booking a couple for a stay in September when the doorbell rang. Expecting it to be Trish, Emily threw open the door with a smile. "Are you looking forward to—" she began, then stopped.

Instead of Trish, Emily found herself looking at Roger Newton. Roger was wearing jeans and a plaid Oxford shirt with silver cufflinks rather than the Oak Hill Police Department uniform Emily was used to seeing him in. Emily had two fleeting thoughts: Roger looked very handsome, and his cufflinks matched the hair at his temples.

Those thoughts were quickly replaced by concern when Emily realized Roger looked even more serious than usual. "Officer Newton," she said guardedly. "Would you like to come in?"

Roger leaned forward slightly, then answered, "Sounds like you have guests. Why don't we sit out here on the porch?"

He has something bad to tell me, and he doesn't want my guests to overhear.

Feeling a cold tingle as fear rose inside her, Emily dutifully followed Roger outside and joined him on the swing.

Roger cleared his throat, and when he spoke, his eyes were fixed on the horizon instead of on Emily. "Miss Emily, I'm here as a friend. First, I want you to know you're not a suspect in Thornton Daley's murder."

Emily wasn't sure what the proper response was to a statement like that, and she finally settled for a quiet, "Thank you."

"However," Roger continued, finally turning to Emily with a worried look, "you should also know we found some evidence today. It doesn't make you look good."

Emily wanted to tell Roger the suspense was killing her and to just get to the point, but she knew it wouldn't do any good. Roger seemed to think he was taking the polite, gentle approach to sharing his news.

He cleared his throat again, then said, "The police found a discarded Grainy Day box this morning. It was shoved under some fallen branches in the very back corner of Memorial Garden. There were biscuit crumbs in it, as well as traces of peanuts."

Emily blanched. The information really wasn't that surprising, since everyone already knew it was a Grainy Day biscuit that had delivered the lethal dose of peanuts, but knowing the Oak Hill Police had found additional evidence was still jarring.

"That's not the worst part," Roger continued. He gently put a hand on Emily's arm. "They were your biscuits, Miss Emily. The box had Eternal Rest's name written on it."

Emily shook her head. "That can't be right. When I have a houseful of guests, Trish delivers a dozen biscuits to me, along with the rest of my order. I've received my complete order every evening, so they can't have been my biscuits."

"And yet, the ones found at the cemetery were clearly meant for you," Roger countered.

"What does that mean?" Emily asked, feeling a rising panic. She brought her hands together in her lap, nervously clasping and unclasping them. "Was someone trying to kill one of my guests instead of Thornton, but the boxes got mixed up?"

Even as she spoke, Emily knew that wasn't the right answer. She let out a shaky breath and sat back in the swing. "Do you think someone is framing me for Thornton's murder?"

15

Roger hesitated. "We don't know if someone is trying to frame you for Thornton's murder, or if it's just a big coincidence," he said.

That feeling of panic was stronger now, and Emily curled her hands into fists and pressed them to her mouth. She didn't need to point out Vic's editorial had also made her seem like a suspect. Between the biscuit box and Vic's veiled accusation, Emily knew things might be looking worse for her than for Trish at the moment.

Unless the police think we went in on it together.

Emily's breathing became rapid and shallow, and she felt Roger's hands against hers, gently pulling them down and away from her face. "Miss Emily, look at me." He leaned toward Emily so she had no choice but to comply. "Remember, I started this conversation saying you aren't a suspect."

Emily nodded feebly. "I guess I forgot," she said, her voice barely above a whisper. She focused on slowing her breathing, feeling comforted by Roger's words as well as his reassuring grip on her hands.

"First of all, I know you're not the type to kill someone, especially not over something as silly as a bad review. Second, we know Eternal Rest has been full lately. How could you possibly sneak out, kill someone, dig a grave, stash the body, and get back here, all before your guests noticed? Third"—here Roger paused and looked embarrassed—"Detective Hernandez still has the login information you gave him for your security cameras. He took a peek at the footage from Monday night, and of course, no one came or went from Eternal Rest."

Emily looked at Roger incredulously. "Is that even legal?"

"If you want to get technical," he began, shifting his gaze away from Emily, "well, you see—"

"It's okay," Emily interrupted. "I gave Danny the login information to help with one murder case, so I don't mind that he's using it to help with another, especially if the footage helps clear me of any suspicion. Speaking of Danny, why didn't he just call to tell me all this?"

Roger looked embarrassed again, and he ducked his head. "Danny doesn't want you anywhere near this case. He didn't want to tell you about the biscuit box having Eternal Rest's name on it, because he said it didn't affect you, anyway. Plus, I think he figures if you found out about any tie between the murder and you, you'd dive into the investigation on your own. But, you know how gossip travels. I didn't want you to hear it from some unofficial source, and I didn't want you to be caught off-guard if people around town start whispering about you."

Emily sighed dramatically. "They already are. My mom called me this morning with a similar warning, but it was because of that opinion piece in *The Oak Hill Monitor*, not because of the biscuit box. It's been a really long day, Officer Newton."

"Just remember, you have nothing to worry about."

"Unless someone is intentionally framing me. Vic Oberfeld made me look like the one with the most likely motive in that editorial of his."

Roger smirked. "Are you accusing Vic of framing you?"

Emily thought it was possible, but there was no point speculating about it with Roger. Instead, she ignored his question and said, "I really appreciate you taking the time to come talk to me. You look like you're on your way out for the night."

"I'm taking my wife out for our anniversary. Speaking of which, I'd better get going. I told her I wouldn't be gone long, and we've got dinner reservations."

Emily wished Roger a happy anniversary, even though she hadn't even known he was married. She walked him to the edge of the porch, thanking him again, then collapsed onto the swing as soon as his car turned onto the road.

There were so many thoughts swirling through Emily's mind that she wasn't even sure where to start. Since Roger had assured her she wasn't a suspect—and her security cameras proved she hadn't been sneaking out of Eternal Rest at night—she was feeling more curious than concerned about the biscuit box. If she was being framed, then the attempt had already been foiled. Hopefully, it was just a coincidence. A very strange, suspicious coincidence.

Roger's visit had also renewed Emily's frustration with Danny. She didn't understand why he hadn't simply called to tell her Eternal Rest had a connection to the case. Surely he knew she would have heard about it eventually.

Not wanting to get upset over his behavior again, Emily pulled her cell phone out of her pocket and called Trish. "Hey," Emily said when Trish answered, "I know I'm about to see you, but this can't wait." Quickly, she told Trish about the box the police had found, and when she was finished, Trish uttered the longest "umm" Emily had ever heard.

"Hang on, I'm thinking back," Trish said. There was a long silence, punctuated now and then by little mumbles and a "huh" or two. Finally, Trish began to speak slowly and thoughtfully. "I label my orders, so clearly that box had been earmarked for Eternal Rest. At the end of each day, I load up my car with your order, any other deliveries I might be making, and all of the day's leftovers. The leftover bags and boxes aren't labeled, but I drop those items at the food bank. I go there before I go to your house."

Trish paused again before continuing. "On Monday evening, I distinctly remember unloading at the food bank, then getting back to my car and seeing that your order was too small. You've had the same order for the past two weeks, and I can just tell at a glance if it's not right. I pawed through it and realized the biscuits weren't there, so I went back into the food bank and told them I'd accidentally given them one box too many. Of course, they just grabbed whatever biscuit box was in easiest reach, and I didn't care whether or not your name was on it."

"That would mean someone took the box labeled for me from the food bank, laced the biscuits inside with peanut dust, and gave it to Thornton," Emily said.

"I'm going to call them right now to ask if they remember who got that box." Trish hung up in such a hurry, she didn't even say goodbye.

Even though she had already taken a nap, Emily felt like she needed another one. She was emotionally exhausted after such a long day and so many strange revelations. Hoping dinner would perk her up a bit, she went inside and headed straight for the kitchen.

Emily made it through both cooking and eating dinner without a single phone call, text, or unexpected visitor. The peace and quiet were a welcome change of pace, and she felt a little more energized as she followed her guests out the front door shortly before eight o'clock.

Trish was already waiting for everyone at Grainy Day,

and she had propped the back door open to let in some fresh air. Emily saw Trish's pinched expression as soon as she stepped out of her car. After making quick introductions, Emily said under her breath, "What's wrong? Has Thornton's ghost caused trouble again?"

"No," Trish answered, just as quietly. "The food bank said the box of biscuits they handed back to me was the only one in the delivery. There was no box there for anyone to take, let alone one that was labeled for you."

"Then how did someone get their hands on it? Do you think the murderer snuck into the bakery and stole it?"

"I think it's more likely someone stole it from my car: I leave the trunk open when I'm loading up, and I always make a few trips between the kitchen and the car. It would have been so easy for someone to stroll past and snag a box while I was in the kitchen, gathering up the next armload."

Emily suppressed a shiver. That meant Trish might have missed seeing Thornton's killer by mere seconds. "The killer either saw an opportunity and took it, or they had watched your bakery enough to know your routine," Emily said. "And if it's the latter, did they purposely take baked goods marked for me, or was it just chance that they grabbed my box of biscuits?"

Trish shook her head solemnly. "I want answers, but we just seem to get more questions. I'm sorry, Emily. I know you need Clint at Eternal Rest, but he's going to be here at the bakery with me until this murder is solved. I'm not coming here alone until we catch this killer."

"Your safety is more important than answering the phone," Emily said firmly. Inwardly, she was disappointed at the idea of losing yet another assistant, but that only fueled her desire to find Thornton's killer as soon as possible. Once the murder was solved, Clint could resume his job at Eternal Rest.

Sage arrived while Emily's guests were setting up their video cameras in the kitchen. She had a large travel mug in one hand and her bag of séance tools in the other. "I may not be much help tonight," she told Emily. "I'm worn out."

"Any help is appreciated," Trish said, who walked up at that moment. She reached out and plucked the cup out of Sage's hand. "I'll make some fresh coffee."

Soon, Marlon told Emily he and his team were ready. Emily, Sage, and Trish stood behind the group, who were seated in a semi-circle on the floor of the kitchen. Sage was letting the ghost hunters start things off, promising to step in if their efforts didn't yield any results.

Emily had given Marlon a list of names to ask Thornton's ghost about. Once the team's video cameras and tape recorders were on, Trish turned off the lights, and Marlon started addressing the empty space over the kitchen stove. "Thornton Daley, are you here with us?" Marlon called. "We want to help you find your killer. Were you killed by" —he flicked on a flashlight and consulted the list—"Jimmy Stanton? If you were, make a noise, talk into our tape recorders, or move something."

"Thornton may not know who gave him those biscuits," Emily told Marlon. "Remember, Thornton still thinks Trish killed him, since she baked them."

Emily could barely see Marlon nodding his head, and soon he said clearly, "Do you think Jimmy Stanton might have wanted to kill you?"

Emily wasn't surprised when nothing happened, since she was convinced of his innocence.

"Could Mercedes O'Brian have killed you?" Marlon continued. "We understand your partnership with her ended badly."

The room remained quiet, even when Marlon asked about Vic Oberfeld.

"Can I try?" Maggie sounded nervous, but Marlon told his sister to ask whatever she liked.

"Mr. Daley," Maggie said, "are there any restaurant owners who might have wanted you dead?"

There was a loud thud followed by the sound of breaking glass, and everyone jumped. Several of the ghost hunters turned on their flashlights, and the bright beams began to sweep around the dark kitchen. "There!" Marlon shouted, pointing his flashlight toward a framed newspaper article that had fallen to the floor. It was easy to see the blank spot on the wall where it had been hanging, surrounded by other framed newspaper clippings.

Trish huffed out her breath and grumbled, "Of course he pulled that one down from the wall. The article says positive things about the bakery and calls my biscuits 'an airy little bite of heaven.' I'll sweep up the glass once the lights are back on."

"Good job, Maggie!" Marlon said proudly. "I think that's a yes from Thornton! There's at least one restaurant owner with a big enough grudge against him that they might kill over it."

"I just thought we could start with broad questions, and narrow it down from there," Maggie answered, her voice sounding more excited than nervous. "And like you just said, there has to be at least one." Maggie turned her attention to the open space of the kitchen. "Mr. Daley, are there more than ten restaurant owners who might have wanted to kill you?" When there was no response, she said, "Are there nine?"

Maggie worked her way down from ten, but each time, she was met only with silence. Finally, she was down to her final question. "Is there one restaurant owner who might have wanted to kill you?"

There was a loud ding and a metallic sound, and Emily

didn't need a flashlight to know it was the cash register drawer popping open.

Everyone in the room gasped but remained otherwise quiet, except for Sage, who said excitedly, "Oh! Money! This is about money! Thornton is channeling the image of a stack of cash!"

Emily immediately thought of her least-favorite guest at Eternal Rest, Jaxon Knight-MacGinn, who had been killed while delivering a duffel bag full of money to someone. "Blackmail!" she shouted excitedly.

"I don't know about blackmail, but it is possible Thornton owed someone money, and when he couldn't pay up, they killed him," Sage suggested. "Or, maybe, Thornton was the one getting money. Someone could have been paying him to give their restaurant a good review."

Trish snorted derisively. "Except Thornton never gave good reviews. It's more likely a restaurant owner would pay him not to write a review at all. Maybe I should have tried that before he wrote about Grainy Day!"

"I think Sage's first guess might be the best one," Emily said. "At the funeral today, Trevor and I met Mercedes O'Brian, Thornton's old business partner. Thornton left Mercedes with a stack of bills she couldn't pay on her own when he backed out of their restaurant project. Mercedes definitely had motive, though there could certainly be someone else around Oak Hill who Thornton left in a financial lurch."

"Maggie, you did a great job getting Thornton to communicate," Sage said encouragingly. "Would you like to continue?"

Maggie nodded eagerly, and said loudly, "Thank you, Thornton! Now, can you please give us a sign if the money has to do with your business partner, Mercedes? Did you owe her money? Did you owe someone else money?"

Thornton remained stubbornly silent during the long pauses between each question. Eventually, Sage began to speak in the low, almost monotone voice she used when communicating with spirits. "Thornton, you opened the cash register and showed me a stack of cash. We understand your murder had something to do with money. Can you please give me more details?"

Emily turned to watch Sage, even though her face was barely visible in the pale glow from the streetlights shining dimly through the bakery windows. Sage usually had a relaxed look when she was trying to channel a message from a ghost, but this time, she had a strained expression, her eyes squeezed tightly shut and her brow furrowed. "Come on, Thornton, please," Sage said quietly.

After a few more minutes, Sage sighed, and she sounded resigned as she said, "He's so stubborn, and I'm almost wiped out from trying to convince him to talk. He seems hesitant now. I almost feel like he's embarrassed."

"Thanks for trying, Sage," Trish said. "If nothing else, it seems we've convinced Thornton to think about people who had a motive, so he's no longer convinced it was me who killed him."

"His anger toward you has definitely subsided, though I think he might still hold a grudge against your biscuits." Sage gave a tired laugh. "I'm not going to be any more help here. I need sleep."

Emily's guests were eager to continue their work, and Trish immediately told them she was happy to stay with them for another hour or two. Emily wished them all good luck, saying she would walk Sage out before heading home, too.

"Trish is right; we're making progress," Emily said optimistically as she accompanied Sage to her car.

"We are. I just wish I wasn't so tired. I also wish Thornton wasn't so stubborn! A lot of times, I get the impression a ghost wants to communicate, but they don't know how. Thornton, however, is guarded. I think he could spill the beans about that money if he wanted to, but for some reason, he won't."

"None of the possible explanations we came up with were things someone would be proud of," Emily pointed out.

"True."

"Oh, I nearly forgot to tell you!" Emily said as Sage opened her car door. "It's been such a crazy day that it nearly slipped my mind! When I met Mercedes at the cemetery today, I saw this brownish-red color around her, like she was surrounded in shimmering rust. I think it might have been her aura."

Sage's eyes brightened, and she took Emily by both hands. "This is fantastic! Not only does this show that you're becoming more psychically sensitive, but it might also give us some insight about Mercedes. A rusty color like that could indicate repressed anger or frustration."

"She was pretty straightforward about having conflicting feelings regarding Thornton's death."

"And what you saw proves she's speaking the truth. The question is, is she angry enough to kill?"

Emily shook her head. "That I can't tell you, but I'm definitely going to keep her on the potential suspect list."

"Agreed," Sage said as she slid into the driver's seat. "Oh, hey, can you meet us for lunch tomorrow? I've asked Reed and Trevor to join me and Jen at The Depot. It's been a hard week for all of us, so I thought we could all hang out and commiserate."

"I can join you as soon as these ghost hunters check

out. The group coming in tomorrow won't be in until after dinnertime."

"We'll be there at noon, if I'm not still in bed!" Sage gave Emily a wave and shut her car door.

Emily drove home, wondering how in the world they were going to narrow down the list of suspects based on the little insight Thornton's ghost had shared with them. "If we could just look at his bank records, maybe we could find large amounts coming in or out of an account, and trace it to our murderer," Emily said out loud as she turned into her driveway.

The response to that rose in her mind, like she was having a conversation with herself: *Danny would have that information.*

Yes, Detective Hernandez would have access to Thornton's financial records, and Emily knew he would take anything she said about a ghost seriously, but that would mean actually talking to him. Even Roger was aware of how anxious Danny was to keep Emily out of this investigation, and she didn't want to go barging into his office unannounced to admit she'd been doing the one thing he had told her not to.

Emily thought about texting him the information, since any negative response from Danny might sting a little less if it was in typed form, but that still seemed like a bad idea. She also considered contacting Mercedes O'Brian directly, thinking it might be possible to glean some insight from her. While Emily didn't expect Mercedes to simply admit to murder, she might learn something else that would be useful.

Then again, Emily reminded herself, Danny would probably hear about that meeting, and then she would really be in trouble with him.

It was two o'clock in the morning, long after Emily had heard her guests return to the house, and even long after the house had quieted down again, before she finally fell asleep.

On Sunday morning, Emily was still having an internal debate about whether or not she should share the news about the money with Danny. She was able to push it out of her mind when her guests came down for breakfast, saying they would be checking out shortly after they ate so they could get in as much daytime driving as possible.

Emily thanked her guests many times on their way out the door, but their gratitude toward her was every bit as enthusiastic. Their only disappointment was not being able to stay to try again with Thornton's ghost.

Once they were gone, Emily's mind went right back to what she was thinking of as her "Danny dilemma" while she headed upstairs to clean the guest rooms. By the time Emily needed to get to The Depot for lunch, the rooms were neat and tidy, but her mind was as cluttered and confused as it had been since the night before.

Lunch wasn't quite the welcome break from reality Emily had been expecting. Instead, it was a chance for everyone to rehash the events of the week. Jen, who hadn't been present for the most exciting parts, listened eagerly, and even Reed seemed engrossed in Sage and Emily's retelling of the investigation at the bakery. Trevor was more subdued than the others, but Emily expected that was due to losing his father.

Emily was just beginning to ask her friends for advice on what to do with the information they had gleaned from Thornton's ghost, and whether she should relay it to Detective Hernandez, when a solution presented itself.

The first thing Emily noticed was a white cowboy hat bobbing across the patio. The second thing she noticed was a pile of platinum-blonde hair gliding next to it. The cowboy hat, Emily knew without looking, belonged to Allen Gerson. The hair belonged to none other than Mercedes O'Brian, who walked confidently between the tables, seemingly unaware of the diners staring after her. Emily decided Mercedes was either used to being part of the town gossip thanks to her history with Thornton, or she just didn't care.

Mercedes's brother, Wynn, followed in their wake, moving slowly while looking at the other diners with something like disdain. Despite the heat—and the fact there was no funeral to attend this time—he was still dressed in an impeccable tailored suit. Emily idly thought that few people in Oak Hill could pull off a burnt-orange suit and paisley tie, but Wynn managed to do it.

"I'm going to go talk to her," Emily blurted, rising from her chair. She had dismissed the idea of talking directly to Mercedes earlier for fear of getting into more trouble with Detective Hernandez, but the opportunity was too good to pass up, and Mercedes being at The Depot the same time as Emily seemed like some kind of sign. At least, that was how Emily chose to take it.

"Whoa, there," Reed said, his hand darting out to catch Emily's wrist. "Are you about to ask her if she killed Thornton?"

"No, of course not. I'm just going to ask her a few questions about money," Emily said.

"I'll go with you," Sage volunteered.

Soon, Sage and Emily were approaching Allen, Mercedes, and Wynn, who were already on the sidewalk and beginning to walk away from The Depot.

"Mr. Gerson!" Emily called, making sure she sounded friendly. "We've really got to stop running into each other like this!"

"Well, this is a surprise," Allen answered as he turned and recognized Emily. "And it's Allen, remember? I didn't realize you were here, as well. Have you met Mercedes and Wynn?"

"We met yesterday," Emily said, smiling politely at them before introducing Sage.

Mercedes pulled a pair of large round sunglasses out of her purse and slid them on. Even though Emily could no longer see her eyes, she knew by the tilt of Mercedes's head that she was gazing toward the table in the front window where Emily and Sage's friends were seated. "Emily, right?" Mercedes asked. "Tell me about that good-looking sexton. Is he single? I wanted to ask yesterday, but it seemed inappropriate since we were at the cemetery."

Emily couldn't help her laughter. "You'll have to ask him," she admitted. "I've been trying to find that out myself, but he's being mysterious about it." Emily knew Reed was still talking to one of her longtime guests, the artist Kat Mason, but he refused to say whether it was more than a friendship.

"I'll do that," Mercedes said, her bright-red lips turning up in a little smile. "And how long have you and your boyfriend been together? Trevor, I believe his name was."

Emily could feel her cheeks flush as she answered haltingly, "Oh, Trevor and I are just friends."

Next to her, Emily could hear Sage talking about ghosts with Allen, while Wynn stared silently at Sage's pink hair, his mouth slightly agape. "Why stop with the biscuits?" Sage was saying. "If your new building is haunted, maybe we could team up for a promotional event where I communicate with your ghost. It could be a ticketed event: dinner and a séance!"

Emily suspected Sage was distracting Allen and Wynn to give her a chance to question Mercedes, so she didn't waste any time. "Rumor has it Thornton backed out of your partnership and left you in a financial mess," Emily said sympathetically. "Was he really that bad?"

Mercedes nodded emphatically. "Whatever you're picturing, it was worse. He made all these big promises, saying he'd pay his fair share and that I should move forward with our plans. At first, he was true to his word, so I had no reason not to trust him. Then, when the first really big payments started coming due, he just bailed. He tried to pin the blame on me, saying I was a bad manager and should have never gotten us so deep into debt. I had to file bankruptcy. It ruined my reputation, too. Even if I'd had the money, I doubt anyone in Oak Hill would have wanted me as their business partner."

"I'm so sorry," Emily said sincerely. Even though it was exactly what Etta-Jane had told her at the funeral, it was still shocking to hear it from Mercedes herself.

"It ruined my dream of ever opening a restaurant," Mercedes continued. "It took me years to recover financially, and no bank would give me the loan I needed to try again. That's why I'm talking to Allen. I've saved up enough that I can at least invest a little bit in a place, which is the next best thing for me. And, of course, it helps that he's not from here, so he's not as afraid of working with me as everyone else in this town."

"If his barbecue is half as good as he's been promising, then it's a smart venture for you," Emily said.

"It will be delicious," Allen said, apparently overhearing Emily's remark. "I've just asked Sage if you two would like to come see the place. Mercedes and I are heading there now, and since I'm convinced it's haunted, I'd love to know whether you two sense anything."

"I have to get to work. I have clients this afternoon," Sage said, her disappointment clear. "However, I think Emily should go. It will be good practice for her growing skills!" Sage winked at Emily, and Emily had to wonder whether the "growing skills" Sage was referring to meant her mediumship abilities or her amateur sleuthing.

Emily smiled, trying not to look too excited. There was no way she was going to miss an opportunity to spend more time with Mercedes. "I'd love to," she said.

Allen gave her the address, and then Emily returned to the table, flagged down a server so she could pay, and told her friends her plan. Everyone wished her luck, except Trevor, who threw cash on the table and said, "I'm coming with you. Don't even think about arguing with me."

"I know better than that," Emily said, smiling gratefully. "I'll drive."

The building Allen had found for the restaurant was only a five-minute drive south of town, but it stood alone along a two-lane road, surrounded by pine trees. It looked like an old service station, and its sun-bleached brick exterior was punctuated by large garage doors made of glass panes. Faded paint on the side of the building read *Last Gas For Ten Miles!*

Allen unlocked the front door and ushered everyone

inside proudly. "We've just about finished the dining room. I'm waiting on a few pieces of decor still."

The polished wooden booths and tables gleamed in the sunlight coming through the garage doors, and the exposed brick walls gave the place a warm feeling. Emily and Trevor both offered their praise while Allen and Mercedes beamed at them.

Emily felt a prickle against the back of her neck, and she recognized it as the feeling she got when someone was staring at her. She turned around slowly, but she saw only the brick wall behind her, which was adorned with various newspaper articles. Not wanting to alert the others to her feelings, especially since she didn't know if it was paranormal or just her imagination, Emily strolled toward the wall as casually as she could, pretending she was interested in looking at the articles.

Emily's feigned interest turned into real appreciation when she saw one of the stories was from *The Atlanta Journal-Constitution*. "Allen," she said, looking at him over her shoulder, "does the list of restaurants in this story include one of yours?"

"It sure does," Allen said proudly. "I used to co-own a barbecue place down in Covington, and we were good enough to make the paper's list of the best hidden gems near Atlanta."

"That's no small feat! Now I'm even more excited to eat here," Emily said, impressed. She looked at a few more of the articles on the wall, which all included praise for the barbecue restaurant in Covington. "You got some great reviews for that place! Congratulations."

Allen tipped his hat appreciatively. "Thank you. Since this place is brand new, I figured I'd brag a little by putting these up. It feels a bit egotistical, but Mercedes says it will reassure the diners they're in good hands."

When Allen offered to give Emily and Trevor a tour of

the kitchen, they both enthusiastically agreed and began to follow him toward the double doors that led to the back of the restaurant.

As they walked, Emily asked Mercedes, "Why didn't your brother join us?"

Mercedes swept her arm to indicate the dining area. "Wynn wouldn't be caught dead here. He thinks barbecue is beneath him."

"I'm sure he wouldn't want to get barbecue sauce on one of his nice suits," Emily said playfully.

"That's true. Also, there's no valet service here, no coat check, and no exotic menu items with names no one can pronounce." Mercedes held up a hand to mimic holding a drink, one pinky sticking out. "He grew out of Oak Hill a long time ago."

"Where does he live now?"

"New York. He's part owner of an Asian-fusion restaurant up there, and it's a lot fancier than anything we have here in Oak Hill."

"Wow, that's great for him," Emily said. She meant it, but she also thought it explained a lot about why he would barely even look at Emily and Sage. Clearly, Wynn thought he was above both barbecue and Oak Hill residents. Struck with another thought, Emily said, "It must be expensive to open a restaurant in New York."

Mercedes nodded. "The rent alone is astronomical. Wynn worked his way up to that level of dining, starting with a little place in Atlanta twenty years ago."

"Why didn't you invest in his restaurant instead of Allen's?" Emily asked.

Mercedes paused, and when Emily glanced at her, she could see the way her jaw tightened. "He wouldn't let me," Mercedes said eventually. "After what happened with Thornton, he says I'm bad luck."

Mercedes hurried her pace to open the door to the

kitchen, waving Emily through. Emily found herself in a gleaming new kitchen outfitted with stainless steel appliances and work surfaces. Out of the corner of her eye, she saw Mercedes holding the door for Trevor.

Mercedes was surrounded by a shimmering, rust-red light.

18

Emily told Trevor about seeing Mercedes's aura for a second time as they drove back to town together. Trevor looked at Emily teasingly. "What color is mine? And does it set off my eyes?"

"I haven't seen yours," Emily said seriously, too lost in thought to even realize Trevor was joking with her.

Trevor leaned slightly forward in the passenger seat, peering at Emily's face. "Tell me what you're thinking about."

"Right before I saw her aura, I got a creepy feeling of being watched," Emily said. "I turned around, but there was nothing there."

"Allen said he thinks the place is haunted," Trevor pointed out, "and it's clear your ability to see and sense what most of us can't is getting stronger."

"I guess I could have sensed a resident ghost. It also could have been my imagination. Still, I feel like there's some connection I'm not making. Maybe me feeling watched is somehow related to Mercedes and her anger." Emily sighed. "I can't explain it, other than to say I feel like there's something just beyond my mental reach. It's so close, but I can't figure out what it is."

"You should talk to Sage about this feeling," Trevor

said. "I'm guessing she felt that way when she was learning to control her psychic abilities, too."

"I will." Emily had reached the square, and she pulled into a parking space near Trevor's car. As Trevor started to open the car door, Emily spontaneously reached out and caught his arm. He turned back to Emily, one foot already on the ground outside. "Thank you," she said earnestly.

"For what? Going with you to see the new restaurant?" Trevor looked genuinely confused by Emily's gratitude.

"For not telling me I'm crazy about all this ghost and aura stuff. For supporting me when I want to help a ghost. For not saying I just need to mind my own business."

Trevor pulled his leg back into the car so he could turn his whole body toward Emily. "Has someone told you you're crazy, or that you need to stay away from helping Thornton find his killer?"

"The Oak Hill Police Department has been pretty firm that I should sit this one out."

Trevor actually laughed. "Let me guess: Officer Newton the skeptic doesn't want you talking to Thornton's ghost?"

"Danny the believer doesn't want me getting mixed up in this case. He talked to me like I was a kid who can't stay out of trouble," Emily said angrily. "He thinks I might get hurt."

Trevor's smile disappeared, and Emily could see the concern in his eyes. "He's not wrong. You've had a couple of close calls with previous investigations. I'm sure he just wants to keep you safe."

"He made me feel stupid." Emily knew she was pouting, but it felt good to finally voice her feelings to someone.

"You can be a little stubborn sometimes," Trevor said, a hint of teasing in his voice. "Maybe Danny thought he had to be blunt to get his point across. Not that it worked, since here we are, just wrapping up a chance to hang out with a suspect." Trevor took Emily's hand and squeezed her fingers reassuringly. "Honestly, Emily, none of us wants you to get hurt. Remember, one of my first experiences with you was watching my own dad wave a shotgun toward us. It was scary, but I understand that if you're determined to help these ghosts, then sometimes, you might have a close call. I don't like it, of course, but I understand it."

Emily leaned over and hugged Trevor tightly. "Thanks."

"I'll talk to you soon," Trevor promised.

Emily drove home, feeling physically lighter. It had been a relief to share her frustration about Danny, and Trevor had helped her put the incident in perspective. Danny didn't have the gentlest approach all the time—he had even admitted that in the past, saying he had a hard time switching between being a detective searching for the truth and just being a regular person making conversation —and after talking to Trevor, Emily could see that what mattered wasn't the way Danny had spoken to her, but the concern behind the words. He cared enough about her that he wanted to keep her safe.

Once she got home, Emily considered calling Sage just as Trevor had advised, but she also knew Sage was likely with a client at Seeing Beyond. Instead, Emily sent her a text, asking her to call when she was free.

The afternoon was quiet, and even the phone seemed to be ringing less. For Emily, it was blissful. She did a few things around the house, then indulged in one of her favorite activities: a Sunday afternoon nap on the parlor sofa. It was getting late in the day for a nap, but Emily didn't care. Since she had been fully booked lately, it had been weeks since she had gotten to lounge on the sofa with a book until drifting off for a while. It was the third day in a row she had fit in a nap, and she couldn't help but think of Sage, who had started doing the same.

I guess we're just getting old.

Emily was in the middle of a strange dream, asking a man in a black suit for directions to the nearest dead body, when she heard the sound of knocking. She looked over her shoulder and saw a silver casket, thinking whomever was inside must be the one knocking. When the sound persisted, Emily slowly began to realize the sound wasn't coming from a casket but from her front door. She woke up slowly, feeling disoriented.

"Just a minute!" Emily called loudly. She sat up and pulled her light-brown hair out of her ponytail, which had gotten messy during her nap. She hastily ran her fingers through her hair, then gathered it up again into a neat—neater, at least—ponytail. Before going to the door, Emily stopped to look at her reflection in a small mirror above a side table in the parlor. Her face looked fine, but her blue button-down shirt was rumpled. She tugged at the hem and tried to make herself look more presentable.

Emily opened the door wide, a polite smile in place, and froze as she realized her visitor was Danny Hernandez. Danny's usually handsome face was marred by a frown. He fixed his brown eyes on Emily and said tersely, "We need to talk."

Emily felt like her heart was rising into her throat as she stepped back and waved Danny inside. He walked quickly past Emily and right into the parlor, where he sat down stiffly in one of the wingback chairs. Emily followed warily and asked, "Can I get you a sweet tea or anything?"

"No, thank you," Danny said, his tone still clipped.

Emily slowly sat on the sofa, purposely choosing the end farthest from the chair Danny was sitting in. She reminded herself Danny's heart was in the right place, even if his delivery wasn't very polished. Readying herself for another warning about staying out of trouble, Emily looked at Danny evenly and said, "What would you like to talk about?"

Danny's eyebrows knit together, and his lips formed a thin line. In that one look, Emily could sense his disappointment, anger, and even fear. "You have been seen talking to suspects in the Thornton Daley case twice in the past two days," Danny said. His voice was so quiet Emily had to lean forward to hear him.

Emily's apprehension was replaced with slight confusion. "Are you talking about Vic Oberfeld and Mercedes O'Brian?"

"Obviously."

Emily sat back and crossed her arms. "What, do you have spies keeping tabs on me?"

Danny's shoulders jerked slightly at the accusation, but his gaze never left Emily's. "You know how this town talks."

"Hopefully, your spies told you both Vic and Mercedes approached me and my friends at Thornton's gravesite yesterday. I didn't search out the meeting with either one of them. Vic said a lot of mean things about me in his editorial yesterday, as I'm sure you saw, so I would have preferred to avoid talking to him altogether. As for Mercedes, I didn't even know she existed before the funeral. Then, today, I just so happened to run into her at The Depot."

And then I followed her and Allen out to the new barbecue restaurant, Emily added silently, *but if Danny doesn't know about that, there's no need to tell him.*

"And then you went to that new restaurant on the edge of town with her."

Ouch. His spies are good.

Now it was Danny's turn to cross his arms. "You've also been spending a lot of after-hours time at Grainy Day Bakery."

"Don't tell me Trish is still a suspect, too!" Emily said, startled.

Danny gazed at Emily silently for a moment, then said, "Sage has been there, too."

Emily threw up her hands and looked away. All of her previous hurt and anger had returned, but this time, it was even stronger. Danny trusted her so little he had people keeping an eye on her.

Worse, Emily realized, Danny had every right not to trust her. Despite his warnings, she was still trying to find Thornton's killer. At first, she had simply been eager to clear Trish's name and get the ghost out of her bakery. Somewhere along the line, Emily had become interested in helping Thornton.

Emily's eyes began to sting, and she shut them to try to hold back the tears she knew were coming. She bit her bottom lip in an effort to keep her composure, but it didn't work. She started to cry as shame welled up inside her.

Danny was by Emily's side in an instant, his arm around her shoulders. "Emily, I'm so sorry! I didn't mean to make you cry! I'm upset because you keep putting yourself in situations that could be dangerous, and I'm worried you're going to get hurt or worse. Vic could ruin your reputation by turning your completely innocent comments to him into something sinister. What if Mercedes had been trying to get you in an isolated place today so she could threaten you or hurt you? What if you were being watched at the bakery?"

"Trish didn't kill him," Emily said, gulping.

"It's unlikely."

"And that means Thornton's killer is still out there. You know how much helping ghosts means to me, Danny." Emily wiped her hands across her cheeks.

"I do." Danny's arm slid from Emily's shoulders, and he clasped his hands together as he leaned forward and rested his elbows on his knees. He stared out the window. "I'm sorry, Emily. It's just that I feel… I realize I'm overly protective of you. In my urgency to keep you safe, I came off like a jerk. And now I've made you cry."

Emily laughed weakly. "I'm not crying because of the way you've been treating me this past week. Well, maybe a little," she admitted. "I was angry at you for talking to me like I was a nuisance and for treating me like a child, but I'm crying because I realize you were totally justified in not trusting me. You begged me to stay out of this case, but I dove right in, anyway. You've been so willing to let me participate in the past two murder investigations, and you did nothing but give me chances to prove myself. Then, the first time you asked me to take a step back, I repaid your faith in me by going against your wishes. I'm the one who owes you an apology. I'm sorry, Danny."

Danny turned his face to Emily, all traces of anger and disappointment gone. He looked a little sad, and there was some of that lingering fear in his expression. "I guess we both needed to apologize." Danny reached out and wrapped both of his hands around one of Emily's, and she realized with a start it was the second time someone had held her hand that day. "From now on, I'll be just as protective of you, but I'll go about it in a better way. I also promise that if I ask you to stay out of an investigation, I'll at least keep you informed about what's happening."

"And if there's a ghost to talk to, I can help with that?" Emily asked hopefully. "That's a lot less dangerous than talking to suspects."

"If you and Sage can safely help me by communicating with a ghost, then I'll support it. Mind that 'safe' part."

"Okay." Emily sniffed one last time as she gave Danny a small smile.

"Okay," he repeated. He lifted her hand to his lips, as if he were sealing a pact.

When Danny looked up at Emily again, she saw something different in his eyes. There was an intensity she hadn't seen in them before. "Emily," he said quietly, his voice wavering slightly.

The doorbell rang before Danny could say another word, and Emily felt a wave of relief as she extracted her hand and rose to get the door.

Danny followed Emily, quietly saying he should head home. It was Trish at the door, armed with baked goods for the next morning, and when she and Danny saw each other, Emily could feel the tension between them.

"Detective Hernandez," Trish said coolly.

"Mrs. Alden," Danny said, his tone even. Emily felt a little sorry for him. She was almost certain he had been about to ask her out or admit to feeling more than merely protective of her, and now he was face-to-face with someone he had questioned as a suspect in a murder investigation. Everything about the situation felt awkward. And, Emily realized, when she had protested Trish's innocence, Danny had only said she was unlikely to be the killer, which meant Trish wasn't quite in the clear yet.

Trish shifted her gaze to Emily. "Everything okay here?" Her implication was clear: she wanted to know if Danny had added Emily to the suspect list.

"Everything is fine," Emily assured her. "Actually, things are better than they were. Danny and I have had a good chat." Out of the corner of her eye, Emily saw the appreciative glance he gave her.

"I'm actually on my way out, so I'll leave you ladies to it." Danny's voice sounded the most normal it had since he had arrived at Eternal Rest, smooth and confident.

Emily thanked him, and he gave her another look that implied there was more he wanted to say. He settled for a simple, "Good night, Emily" before slipping past Trish.

"Do you have a minute?" Trish asked Emily once Danny was off the porch and walking toward his truck.

"My guests won't arrive for another couple of hours. Come on in. You want a glass of wine? I know it's a little early, but…" Emily shrugged.

"Yes, please!" Trish followed Emily to the kitchen, putting down her delivery while Emily got two wine glasses out of the cabinet. "The almond-flour scones are in the smallest box. I also gave you a few extra biscuits since they're my most popular item right now."

Emily was planning to go to the parlor, but Trish sank down into one of the chairs at the little wooden table in the kitchen instead. Emily sat down at the other chair and started pouring as she said, "What did you want to talk about? Did Thornton do something again?"

"He did." Trish nodded, then quickly added, "Nothing bad! No damage this time. He definitely seems to have accepted the fact I didn't kill him, and I think he's trying to communicate."

"Sage said he seems to be withholding information," Emily pointed out.

"Maybe he's trying to give us new clues that don't make him look like the bad guy in all of this. The problem, though, is that I can't figure out what he's trying to say." Trish stopped to take a drink. "It started when I went into the bakery this morning. I found that same framed article on the ground again. Thankfully, this time, there was no glass to break! I actually started thinking the nail might not be stable since that's twice in two days. We all assumed it was paranormal when it fell off the wall last night, but maybe not."

Emily nodded. "You could be right. Still, the timing was remarkable."

"Agreed. Anyway, I hung it back up and didn't really think about it for a while. I figured I'd be slammed again, so I wanted to bake up a few extra batches of biscuits before I opened."

"How was business today, anyway?"

"Not as busy as yesterday, which is actually a good thing. I sold out of everything, but today wasn't nearly as stressful for me."

Emily laughed. "Thornton gave you a bad review all those years ago, and now he's making you the most popular place in town!"

"Oh, I've started talking to him while I bake, just in case he's listening, and I've already thanked him several times!" Trish leaned forward, one eyebrow raised. "Here's the really weird part: I think Thornton was trying to help me bake today!"

Emily laughed until she saw Trish's expression was perfectly serious. "What, was he breaking eggs for you?"

"Not quite. I had rolled out the biscuit dough, but my phone rang, so I walked away to answer it. When I came back, Thornton had drawn these little circles in the dough, almost like he was trying to cut out the biscuits for me!"

"That's odd. First he did everything he could to keep you from being able to bake, and now he seems to be helping you along. I wonder why?"

Trish shrugged. "No idea. I told him I appreciated the help, but that I could do it on my own, and that newspaper article crashed to the floor again in answer. So, it's probably not just a bad nail. Thornton didn't do anything else the rest of the day. Here, I took a picture of the dough." Trish pulled her cell phone out of her purse and scrolled to the photo.

Emily took Trish's phone to gaze at the little circles in

the dough. They weren't perfectly round, but they were clearly about the size of a biscuit and laid out in neat rows. There was something familiar about the image.

"There it is again," Emily mumbled.

"There what is again?" Trish asked.

"I got a weird feeling earlier today, like my brain is on the brink of making a connection. I feel like there's some piece of information dangling just beyond my grasp. Trevor said maybe it has to do with my developing mediumship abilities. It's like I've got a psychic channel open but not quite tuned in."

"Well, keep fiddling with that dial!" Trish held up her glass and clinked it against Emily's.

Emily's new guests arrived shortly after eight o'clock in the evening. Instead of being ghost hunters, which had been the bulk of Eternal Rest's business lately, this group was three siblings and their spouses, plus their elderly father. One of the guests, a soft-spoken woman named Alicia, immediately brought up the subject of breakfast as soon as Emily had served the group a welcoming round of sweet teas.

"When Mike made the reservation, I think he mentioned I've got a gluten allergy?" Alicia asked. "I saw on your website that you have a lot of goods from a local bakery, but I can't eat anything made with wheat."

"Mike did mention it! Trish, the owner of the bakery, made up some special almond-flour scones for you." Emily smiled, happy she had been able to accommodate a guest this way. Alicia's allergy made Emily think of Thornton's peanut allergy, which only made her think of his review of her breakfasts. Even a year later—and even after his murder—she still felt a stab of resentment about the things he had said. He had told only half the story, making Emily look like a lazy bed and breakfast owner.

And then Thornton's editor had made her look like a potential killer.

Feeling her anger flare again, Emily tried to push all thoughts of it out of her mind. Instead, she chatted with her guests about where they were from and what they wanted to do while they were in town. The subject of ghosts never came up, and Emily realized it was the first time in months guests hadn't started asking about hauntings right away. After some regional press that noted Eternal Rest was a top haunted spot, and of course, plenty of news about the murders that had involved her and her home, Emily was used to guests who either wanted ghosts or true crime. Instead, this family seemed to want an ordinary vacation.

Emily's guests had all flown from their respective towns to Atlanta, meeting up at the airport before getting a rental van to make the trek north to Eternal Rest. After a long day of traveling, they were ready for an early night. The seven of them went upstairs after finishing their drinks, and Emily retreated into the kitchen to get the coffee maker prepared for the next morning. Without her guests as a distraction, her mind went right back to thinking about Thornton's ghost and the mysterious circles he had drawn in the dough. Then she thought about him throwing the newspaper article off the wall two more times, which only made her think of Vic's editorial. That, in turn, just got her angry all over again. It was not a cycle Emily liked being in.

Of all the things in that bakery Thornton could have moved, why that article? Is he trying to indicate someone at the newspaper could have murdered him?

Emily began to think of her strange feeling at the barbecue restaurant in a different way. At the time, she had thought the feeling of being watched was something paranormal. As she thought about Thornton's apparent fixation with the framed article at Trish's bakery, Emily wondered if it wasn't a ghost but the newspaper articles her subconscious was drawn to at the restaurant. Perhaps she had made the newspaper connection then without even realizing it.

If Thornton really was trying to tell them his murder had something to do with the newspaper, then the obvious suspect was already on the list: Vic Oberfeld.

Emily made a noise of disgust. "And that jerk is trying to make me look like the killer!"

Vic's editorial directing attention away from himself and toward others, like Emily, suddenly seemed even more suspicious than it had before. Vic's eulogy at Thornton's funeral, in which he swore to track down his colleague's killer, also seemed like a way for Vic to deflect the attention away from himself and his own motives.

Emily sat down at the kitchen table to call Sage. She wanted to run her theory by Sage before calling Danny to tell him. Emily would rather have her best friend point out a flaw in her logic than send the Oak Hill Police Department down the wrong path. Before Emily even picked up her phone, though, it began to ring.

It was Reed, and he sounded grim as he said, "The police have arrested Jimmy Stanton for Thornton's murder."

"What? They can't actually think he killed Thornton!"

Reed sighed. "Jimmy said he had a good alibi for Monday night, when Thornton was killed. He didn't lie to the police when he said he was at Sutter's that night, but the security camera in the parking lot shows him leaving the bar at ten o'clock. There would have been plenty of time to kill Thornton after that."

"That doesn't mean he did it. There are at least two

other suspects who could have done it, and neither of them are in jail!" Emily had been so focused on Mercedes O'Brian, and so angry at Vic Oberfeld, that she couldn't imagine how anyone could still be considering Jimmy as a suspect. Sweet, affable Jimmy, who had brought her a casserole in the wake of Scott's death.

"Unfortunately, Jimmy had a few drinks and started running his mouth to Sutter. Several other people at the bar confirmed he said a lot of nasty things about Thornton, right before he threatened to make sure Thornton could never steal a woman from him again."

Emily put a hand out to steady herself against the table. "Oh, Reed. The police felt that was enough to arrest him?"

"Yeah. It's the best evidence they've gotten so far." Emily could hear the shock and sorrow in Reed's voice.

"You said before you didn't think Jimmy could be a killer. Do you still believe he's innocent?"

"Don't you?"

Emily closed her eyes and tried to picture Jimmy stealing biscuits out of Trish's car, then lacing them with powdered peanuts to kill Thornton. There was so much planning involved in that, such intent to kill. "I don't believe Jimmy is the one," she finally said. "This isn't a case of Jimmy, or anyone else, simply having a few too many drinks and spontaneously acting on a bad idea. Someone stole those biscuits out of Trish's car late Monday afternoon, hours before Jimmy ever went to Sutter's. Thornton's murder was pre-meditated."

"You're right. I don't know what time the biscuits were stolen, but I sure hope when the police talk to Trish, they find out it happened while Jimmy was still at work. We were at Hilltop on Monday, and we didn't wrap up until a little after five."

Emily almost introduced her theory about Vic,

thinking it might give Reed hope Jimmy's name would be cleared eventually. Instead, she remained silent on the subject, knowing Reed would be worried about the situation no matter what.

After Emily tried her best to reassure Reed it would all turn out okay for Jimmy, she said goodnight and hung up. She again started to call Sage, then stopped herself. Sage had been so tired the past few weeks, and Emily didn't want to risk waking her up if she had already turned in for the night. Usually, Sage was a night owl, but Emily knew that, lately, she had been spending a surprising amount of time in bed.

That meant Emily would have to wait until sometime the next morning before she could call, so she went to bed with her mind still racing.

Emily felt impatient on Monday morning as she prepared breakfast, greeted her guests when they came downstairs, and went through her usual morning routine of reviewing online reservation requests. Emily's guests left at nine, ready to start a day of sightseeing and antique shopping, but Emily worried it was still a little too early to call Sage. Instead, she cleared the dining room table, loaded the dishwasher, and cleaned the guest rooms. By then, it was nearly eleven, and Emily crossed her fingers as she finally called Sage, hoping she wouldn't be with a client.

Sage answered on the first ring, and Emily felt her shoulders relax. She laid out her theory that Thornton was trying to send a message about Vic, adding that her strange feeling at the barbecue restaurant might have been her subconscious—or even her burgeoning psychic abilities—telling her to look deeper into the newspaper angle.

Sage agreed it was a possibility, but she cautioned Emily against jumping to conclusions. "You know how cryptic ghosts can be," Sage said. "While it's certainly possible Thornton was trying to communicate something specific by pulling that article off the wall of Trish's kitchen, it's also possible it was simply the easiest object for him to manipulate."

"Then how would you explain what happened to me at the barbecue place?" Emily countered.

Sage laughed. "You saw Mercedes's aura again! It's entirely possible your experience at the restaurant really was you sensing a ghost there."

"Oh," Emily said, feeling deflated. "I guess that could have been it."

Emily couldn't see Sage's face, but she knew it probably looked exasperated. "Don't hide your excitement," Sage said sarcastically. "You're learning to sense ghosts, and you sound so disappointed about it."

"I'm not disappointed that my mediumship skills are growing," Emily conceded. "The better I get, the more I'll be able to help Scott. I guess I'm so focused on trying to find Thornton's killer that I'm not taking time to appreciate any ghostly friends I'm meeting along the way."

"What are you doing right now?"

"I'm just holding down the fort here, answering phones. My guests are out, and I don't expect them back until this afternoon."

"Good. Let the phone calls go to voicemail for an hour or so. Let's meet at Grainy Day for a little chat with Thornton."

Emily actually thought Sage might be joking, and she pointed out how busy Grainy Day had been since its reopening on Saturday. "How are you going to communicate with Thornton when it will be so crowded and noisy in there?" Emily asked.

"We'll find a quiet corner of the kitchen. If I focus, I

should be able to sense Thornton even though we're not alone."

Emily agreed, and soon, she was in her car, heading for Grainy Day. Sage was already there, waiting for her on the sidewalk. There was a line out the door of the bakery again, but it was shorter than the one on Saturday.

When Emily and Sage walked into the bakery, Trish spotted them while she was filling up one of her most popular specials, a Basket Full of Biscuits. Customers seemed to enjoy the pretty presentation, and they had a basket to keep after all the biscuits were gone.

Trish paused and glanced toward Emily and Sage, waving a biscuit as she asked, "You here for me or for Thornton?" A few customers who overheard looked over in surprise at the name.

"Thornton," Sage said airily, sounding totally unconcerned about the stares she and Emily were getting. "We just have a couple of quick questions for him."

Trish jerked her head over her shoulder. "Help yourself."

Sage and Emily found a little corner of the kitchen that was out of sight from the customers in the front of the bakery. The voices still carried to where they were, but at least there was some amount of privacy. Sage put her purse down, closed her eyes, and took several deep breaths.

Emily followed Sage's lead, and the din of conversation seemed to grow quieter as she focused her attention on their small part of the kitchen. "Thornton," Sage said quietly, "will you please join us? I have questions, and your answers might help us figure out who killed you."

There was a banging noise behind Emily, and she whirled around as she opened her eyes. The same framed article that Thornton's ghost had been throwing to the ground was now sitting on the countertop, about six feet away from the wall where it normally hung. "Was that there already, or did Thornton just move it?" Emily turned back to Sage, who cracked one eye open to look.

"That wasn't there before," Sage said confidently.

Emily picked up the article, which was from *The Oak Hill Monitor* and announced the grand opening of Grainy Day Bakery. There were a few paragraphs about the bakery and Trish herself, along with a photo of Trish holding up a tray of croissants and smiling proudly.

"Thank you, Thornton," Sage called. She shut her eyes again. "Now that we know you're here, I have a very important question for you: do you think Vic Oberfeld could have killed you?"

After a few moments, Sage said, "Did Vic Oberfeld have a reason to kill you?"

Minutes went by in silence, and Emily again became aware of the sound of customers. Suddenly, Sage gasped quietly, then said in an excited voice, "Oh, thank you, Thornton! Well done! Can you be more specific?"

Emily desperately wanted to know what Thornton had done to please Sage, but she also knew not to interrupt the psychic conversation the two were apparently having. After a few more minutes, Sage said in her normal voice, "Thornton is done. I can't get anything more from him."

"What did he say to you?" Emily asked, opening her eyes.

"He didn't say anything, but he showed me money again. Then, he showed me newsprint. I couldn't read any of the words, but he was certainly indicating a newspaper. I couldn't get more out of him than that. What could the cash possibly have to do with Vic? Or anyone at the newspaper, for that matter?"

"Vic was Thornton's boss," Emily noted. "Maybe they were having a disagreement about salary. Thornton could have been asking for more, but Vic refused."

"Whatever the answer is, your hunch that the newspaper is somehow tied into the investigation was right. That means your feeling at that barbecue restaurant really was your intuition talking to you. Great breakthrough, Em!"

"Now that we've confirmed that part, at least, I'm walking to the police station to tell Danny."

Sage sounded surprised as she responded, "I didn't realize you two had been discussing the case."

Emily scoffed. "We hadn't. Until yesterday, Danny had been adamant about keeping me out of it altogether." Emily recounted her recent conversations with Danny, and Sage just chuckled.

"There are a lot of single ladies around here who would like to be under his protection," Sage said. "Consider yourself lucky."

Instead of answering, Emily changed the subject, asking Sage how she was feeling.

"Still tired, but I'm hanging in there," Sage answered, even as she yawned widely. "I've got a client coming in soon, so I'm heading back to the office. I'll walk with you as far as the coffee shop."

Trish was still busy, so Emily merely gave her a quick promise to fill her in that evening when she came by Eternal Rest. Soon, Emily and Sage were out on the sidewalk. They parted ways when Sage veered off to get a coffee at The Stomping Grounds.

Emily felt more and more nervous as she approached the Oak Hill police station, worried Danny might give her that intense look again. She liked Danny, and she completely understood why he was one of the most popular bachelors in town, but she couldn't imagine getting romantically involved with anyone at the moment, even someone as handsome and kind as Danny. Knowing Scott's ghost was still around made the idea even more uncomfortable. How would Scott feel if she got involved with someone else?

Luckily, Danny was all business when Emily was ushered into his office at the back of the ground floor. He was bent over a pile of hand-written notes, and he didn't budge when Emily sat down. "Hi, Danny," she said.

Danny looked up, startled. "Emily! How long have you been sitting there?"

"I just sat down."

Danny sat up straight and stretched his arms over his head. "I've been in here since six this morning. I couldn't sleep because I kept thinking about this case."

"My brain won't stop going over all the information, either. I was actually stopping by to let you know that Sage and Thornton had a little chat just now. I came straight here after leaving the bakery."

Danny leaned forward eagerly. "Did Thornton give you any leads?"

"Possibly." Emily went on to describe the channeled vision of newsprint and money Sage had received from Thornton. She ended with, "We were thinking this might have to do with a salary dispute, or some other kind of money disagreement between Thornton and Vic Oberfeld. We know about their falling out."

Danny was shaking his head before Emily finished talking. "I agree there could be a connection to the newspaper, but I don't think this is about Thornton wanting more money from Vic. As it turns out, Thornton was already getting extra money from somewhere."

"Oh?"

Danny got up and moved to the door of his office. He glanced down the hall briefly before shutting the door and sitting down again. When he spoke, he kept his voice low. "We've been looking at Thornton's bank statements. He deposited one thousand dollars in cash two months ago, on April twenty-fifth. He did the same thing on May twenty-fifth. That means a third deposit would have been expected on June twenty-fifth, the day Thornton's body was found at Oak Hill Memorial Garden."

21

Emily's mind went back to the speculations she and Sage had come up with during the first séance at Grainy Day, when Thornton had opened the cash register and channeled the image of a stack of money. "Thornton might have been blackmailing someone," Emily said, "and that person got tired of coughing up so much cash every month."

"That's our thinking, as well. The question is, what secret did Thornton know that was worth so much money?"

"One of the other possibilities we'd considered is that Thornton wasn't blackmailing someone, but that he was actually being paid off by a restaurant owner in exchange for not giving them a bad review."

Danny looked at Emily thoughtfully. "It's possible, I suppose. In fact, something like that could have been a lucrative racket for Thornton. What if each large deposit was made up of smaller payments he'd collected from multiple restaurants? Everyone knows he gave bad reviews across the board, so it might be worth a little money to keep out of his column. When Vic asked Thornton to stop writing such negative reviews, Thornton staunchly refused. Hmm. We might need to look even further back at his financials. Something like that could have been going on for years."

Emily threw up her hands. "Which means our suspect list just got longer! Now we have to consider restaurants Thornton reviewed as well as the ones he noticeably ignored."

Danny gave Emily a lopsided smile. "We?"

Emily laughed self-consciously. "I mean the Oak Hill Police Department, of course. Not me. Definitely not me."

Danny just raised his eyebrows in response, clearly unconvinced.

"All right, I'm going home, where I can't get myself in any trouble," Emily said, rising from her chair.

"I do appreciate the information about Thornton's ghost, but I'm also glad to know you're going home instead of heading to the newspaper office to start questioning everyone on staff." Danny gave Emily a wink.

"I'm not going near that place," Emily assured him.

As she walked back to her car, Emily thought more about what Thornton's message could mean. Or, more accurately, she thought about what it didn't mean. If Thornton's murder really did have something to do with the newspaper or someone on staff there, then things were looking even better for Jimmy Stanton. Emily couldn't imagine why Jimmy would be paying Thornton money on a monthly basis, anyway.

Halfway back to Eternal Rest, Emily suddenly reached up and pressed her fingertips against her temple as she articulated the questions rising in her mind. "Trish has other newspaper articles hanging on that wall in her kitchen, so why is Thornton focusing on that particular one? What's so special about that article?"

Again, Emily had the feeling the answer was so close, but for some reason, her conscious mind just couldn't make the necessary connection to get there. There must, she decided, be a clue somewhere in that article about the grand opening of Grainy Day.

Emily briefly considered calling Trish and asking her to send over a photo of the article. Instead, Emily made a U-turn and started driving back toward Oak Hill. She wanted to see the story with her own eyes rather than squint at a copy on her phone or computer screen.

When Emily walked into Grainy Day this time, the crowd was smaller, and the line was no longer going out the door. She knew Trish must be happy with the steady, but far less hectic, business.

Emily was already passing the counter before Trish noticed her. "Did you forget something?" Trish called.

"No, I'm just checking something real quick."

Trish didn't respond, since a customer started rattling off an order at that moment, so Emily continued on back to the wall with the framed items. The newspaper article in question, she noticed, was currently hanging exactly where it was supposed to be.

"Is this what you want us to see, Thornton?" Emily asked softly. "Is there something important in this story?"

Emily read through the short article, but she saw nothing that seemed like a possible link to Thornton's murder. The writer mentioned Trish was an Oak Hill native, gave the name of the culinary school she had attended in Atlanta, and included a brief rundown of what the menu would be. In all, it was exactly what one would expect from a nice little announcement about a new business.

Even a second, slower perusal of the article didn't help, and Emily turned her attention to the photo of Trish instead. Since Thornton's ghost had finally accepted Trish's innocence in his death, that seemed to be an unlikely clue.

All that was left was the byline.

The article had been written by someone named Joe Waldrup. Emily didn't recognize the name, but she pulled a pen from her purse and scribbled the name on the palm of her hand.

It was only after Emily finally got back to Eternal Rest that she called Danny to pass along the name, convinced he would somehow know it if she called him from anywhere else. She figured there was no reason to tell him she had made a detour to Grainy Day despite promising to go straight home from the police station.

It was a few hours later when Danny called her back. "Looking for a clue in that article was a good idea, but Joe Waldrup is definitely not a suspect."

"Oh, does he have a good alibi for Monday night?"

"I'm sure the people buried around him at Oak Hill Memorial Garden can vouch that he never left his casket. He died about two years ago."

Emily felt a stab of disappointment that she was back to square one in trying to find a connection between that particular article and the newsprint Thornton had channeled through Sage. She thanked Danny for the update, then hung up, feeling frustrated at Thornton's inability—or stubborn refusal—to communicate with Sage more clearly.

If ghosts could just write out a suspect list for us, it would make things a whole lot easier.

That thought was quickly followed by another. *I should write a list of suspects. There seem to be a lot, and I need to keep track of them.*

Emily sat down at her desk in the parlor and opened a new document on her laptop. She stared at the blank white screen for a moment, then, seized by sudden inspiration, she began to write. What she typed wasn't a suspect list, but a greeting: *Dear Mr. Oberfeld*.

From there, Emily wrote a letter to the editor, defending herself and the breakfasts Thornton Daley had so soundly dismissed. She told Vic how she used to love cooking for her guests, and how she would write down their orders the night before so she would know if they wanted their eggs scrambled or over easy, their bacon extra crispy, or their hash browns served with ketchup. After Scott died, she told Vic, she no longer had time for that joyful ritual every morning, and she no longer smiled when guests told her how delicious their breakfast was. The pride she had taken in such compliments was gone, since the credit was due to others, like Trish. Emily then went on to say how much it had hurt when Thornton had written such mean things about the Continental breakfasts she began to serve following the death of her husband.

I know the grief of losing someone unexpectedly, Emily said in conclusion. *For you to publish a thinly veiled accusation that I might have killed someone is not only untrue, but it is also incredibly callous. Your editorial reminded me of my own loss, and I would certainly never inflict that same loss on anyone else. Thornton Daley hurt my feelings, and so have you, but your insinuations are baseless.*

Emily read through her letter a few times, then found Vic's email address on the newspaper's website. She copied and pasted the letter into an email and hit *send* before she could lose her courage.

That night, Emily slept more soundly than she had in days. She didn't really care whether her letter got published. It didn't even matter whether Vic himself read it. She had defended herself, and that was what counted.

When Emily woke up on Tuesday morning, the review Thornton had written about Eternal Rest was still on her mind but in a different way. She had only ever read it once, and she was beginning to feel it was time to read it again. She needed to make peace with it and with Thornton's low opinion of her breakfasts.

Emily's guests were again out of the house by nine o'clock, this time to take a day-long tour of wineries throughout the North Georgia region. They promised to bring back their recommendations, and Emily was happy to know she would have the freedom to leave the house instead of staying in case her guests came back early. She would ordinarily have an assistant on Tuesdays, and she was missing Clint sorely. Still, she knew it was better for him to be at Grainy Day to help out his mother and to keep an eye on Thornton's ghost.

As soon as she had cleaned up from breakfast and neatened the guest rooms, Emily got in her car and made a beeline for the Oak Hill library. While most of the library's old newspapers had been transferred to microfiche, the librarian informed Emily everything from the past two years was still in print form. Emily was given a box of old newspapers from the time period she remembered the review coming out, and she got to work.

Emily had remembered the month correctly, but she was off in her guess by three weeks. Still, since Thornton's column was almost always in the same spot in the newspaper, it didn't take long for her to find the one about Eternal Rest.

It was just as bad as she had remembered it. Thornton's cold commentary still hurt, but what really angered Emily this time around was the fact Thornton had never even visited Eternal Rest. He had reviewed food he had never even eaten, outside of the baked goods that came from Grainy Day.

The photo accompanying the review showed the front of Eternal Rest, but the dark-blue clapboard looked dark and sinister in black and white. Emily remembered that at the time the review had come out, she had thanked her lucky stars that locals almost never stayed at Eternal Rest. Otherwise, she probably would have seen a dip in business.

Emily stared at the photo, thinking how the way things looked in reality and the way they appeared in photos could sometimes vary wildly. She felt the same tug against her mind that she had felt at both Grainy Day and the barbecue restaurant. There was something, she was certain, telling her to dive deeper into newspaper research. She was missing something, or maybe Thornton's ghost was shouting it at her, but only her unconscious mind had heard him.

With a frustrated sigh, Emily sat back in the hard wooden chair, her head tilting up. The clock on the wall in front of her showed it wasn't quite noon yet. She glanced toward a window that overlooked a grassy area, and she saw a group of kids laughing and blowing bubbles outside. She stared at the bubbles, and that feeling she was close to knowing something became even stronger.

Emily's eyes went back to the clock, then again to the bubbles caught on a breeze outside.

Circles. The clock and the bubbles were making her think of circles.

"Like the circles Thornton drew in the dough," Emily whispered, sitting up straight. Suddenly, she knew why Trish's photo of the dough had seemed so familiar: she had seen one almost exactly like it before, but in black and white.

Thornton's ghost was telling them where to look for a clue. It would be somewhere in a past newspaper, right next to a photo of biscuits all cut out and ready to be moved to a baking sheet.

Emily nearly clapped her hands in her excitement, but she stopped herself when she remembered she was in the middle of a library. Thornton's ghost had pulled the newspaper article off the wall and drawn circles in the dough not in an attempt to communicate two separate messages, but to give them one cohesive message. Emily and her friends needed to look for a newspaper article containing the photo that resembled the circles in the dough.

Since she couldn't clap her hands, Emily settled for a fist pump. This breakthrough helped explain why she had been drawn to the newspaper articles at the barbecue restaurant. She had subconsciously realized Trish's photo of the dough was similar to one she had seen in newsprint.

That, of course, led Emily back around to the same problem she and Sage had discussed previously. If the answer was in one of Thornton's food reviews, it would take ages to go through newspaper after newspaper, looking for the edition that contained the review Thornton's ghost was referring to.

Then again, Emily told herself, there weren't that many places in Oak Hill that made biscuits. She returned the newspapers to their box, thanked the librarian, and stepped outside. Emily paced back and forth as she called Trish, desperately hoping she would pick up.

The call went to voicemail.

With a shrug, Emily decided to simply visit the bakery. Now that she knew what her mind had been trying to tell her all along, she didn't want to wait to start tracking down answers.

Emily had driven nearly halfway to the bakery before she realized she wasn't supposed to be going after leads at all. She had promised Danny she would stay out of the investigation, and she didn't want to feel the same guilt she had during his visit to Eternal Rest.

By the time she pulled into a parking spot in front of the bakery, Emily had come up with a compromise. She was going to tell Danny exactly what she was doing. If he told her in no uncertain terms to turn around and go home, then she would. Hopefully, though, she could convince him to let her do this one small task.

Emily pulled out her cell phone and called Danny. She let out the breath she had been holding when he answered. She hadn't figured out what she would do if her call had gone to voicemail. Confessing her plans over voicemail seemed like a bad idea, but Emily didn't want to go home unless she was explicitly told to.

"Okay," she began, already feeling defensive, "I know I'm supposed to stay out of this murder investigation, but hear me out." Emily explained she had gone to the library simply to look up the review Thornton had written about Eternal Rest. When Danny snorted in disbelief, Emily said, "No, really! Last night, I wrote a letter to the editor. I gave Vic Oberfeld a piece of my mind, and it made me realize I needed to read that review again so I could finally move on from the whole thing."

Emily then went on to explain to Danny how she had made the connection between the circles in the dough and the newspaper, saying she knew she had seen that image before. "I'm at Grainy Day right now, because I was going to ask Trish if she has a copy of Thornton's review of the bakery. I'm guessing the photo of the dough accompanied it."

"I'll take a toasted plain bagel with pimiento cheese," Danny said.

Emily pulled the phone away from her ear and glanced at it. Had Danny even paid attention to what she had just told him? "Are you giving me a food order?" she asked incredulously.

"Yes. If you're insisting on doing this, then I want you to look like you're going into the bakery like any other customer. You can ask Trish about the review when you get to the counter to place your order. Then, you can bring me my bagel, and we'll have a little chat."

Emily couldn't tell if the slight edge in Danny's voice was him feeling frustrated with her again, or if he was laughing at how well his suggestion of a cover story benefitted him. "Are you mad at me?" Emily asked hesitantly.

"No." Danny was quiet for a moment, then he sighed deeply. "Actually, I'm going to meet you there at the bakery. I want to talk to both you and Trish. Will you wait for me outside? I'm buying."

Emily agreed, and Danny promised to be there in five minutes. During the wait, Emily sat on a bench on the sidewalk and watched the steady stream of people going through the front door of Grainy Day. She waved at a woman she recognized just as she heard someone clearing their throat disdainfully. Emily turned her head and saw Vic Oberfeld standing a few feet away. He had a tape recorder in one hand and a reporter's notebook in the other.

"Mrs. Buchanan," Vic said coldly. He walked over and sat heavily on the bench next to Emily. "You've put me between a rock and a hard place."

"How so?" Emily asked.

"If I publish that letter you wrote me, then I come off looking like a bad guy who's pointing the finger at a sweet, innocent widow." Vic smirked. "On the other hand, that letter would fuel the Oak Hill rumor mill nearly as much as Thornton's death. Everyone will want to read it, which means I'll sell more copies. The question is, do I want to risk looking heartless just so I can make more money?"

Emily nodded and said sarcastically, "You're definitely in a tight spot."

"You should have written that letter right after Thornton's review of Eternal Rest came out," Vic said. "I would have published it without hesitation. You make a good point about him not taking the time to understand your situation before passing judgment. Also, since he never actually had breakfast at your B and B, it wasn't a well-informed review."

Emily was so surprised Vic actually agreed with her that it left her silent for a moment. She thought about thanking him for his understanding, then realized his admission still didn't absolve him of accusing her of murder in his editorial. Emily made an effort to keep a resentful tone out of her voice as she asked, "Then why did you let him publish that review in the first place?"

Vic laughed so loudly some people on the sidewalk turned to look at him. "I lost control over Thornton a long time ago. He wouldn't listen to me, but I couldn't fire him. There are people in this town who subscribe to *The Monitor* just to read his weekly vitriol. I don't know what they'll do now that he's gone. And yes, I realize how callous that sounds. I'm sure you know he and I weren't the best of friends."

"I did hear you two had a pretty big falling out, yet you gave the eulogy at his funeral."

"No one else wanted to do it," Vic said, a note of sadness in his voice. "Thornton burned one bridge after another during his life. I realize you were upset by my editorial, Mrs. Buchanan. Frankly, I don't care. I wanted to make the point that there are plenty of people in this town who had reason to dislike Thornton, and for many of those people, the stakes were high. Lost business, financial disasters, even personal relationships gone sour. Hell, I had as much reason as anyone to want him dead."

Vic looked up at that moment and hastily stood. "I'd best be on my way. The deadlines never end."

Before Emily could say goodbye, Vic was gone, hustling down the sidewalk. As Emily watched him, it became obvious why he had left in such a hurry. Danny was walking toward the bench.

Emily rose, her eyebrows arched. "That was a weird conversation," she said. "Vic Oberfeld just managed to say he still thinks I'm a suspect in Thornton's death while also admitting to being one himself."

Danny glanced in the direction Vic had gone. "He's not wrong about being a suspect."

"Well, before you ask, I didn't go chasing after him. He saw me sitting out here and stopped to talk about that letter I sent him."

"Is he going to publish it, then?"

Emily thought for a moment. "Actually, I have no idea. He doesn't even seem sure himself."

"How very mysterious of him." Danny gestured toward the front door of Grainy Day. "Shall we?"

As Emily and Danny went inside the bakery and got behind the few people already in line, Emily turned to Danny with a frown. "How are we supposed to look like regular customers if you're actually here to talk to me and Trish?" she whispered.

"That was my suggestion to keep you safe, when you said you were coming here by yourself," Danny answered, bending his head toward Emily's ear. "Since we're here together, I don't mind this looking like the official police business that it's become."

"Then why are we standing in line?"

Danny smiled at Emily, and he answered at his usual volume, "I'm hungry! I want to have something to eat while we talk."

Emily was curious what Danny could possibly want to discuss with both her and Trish, but he refused to say anything, telling Emily only that it was serious and that he wanted some privacy for the conversation.

It wasn't long before it was Emily and Danny's turn at the counter, and Trish narrowed her eyes when she realized the two of them were there together. After ordering and paying, Danny asked Trish quietly, "Is there somewhere we can talk for a few minutes?"

Trish nodded, but she was still eyeing Danny with distrust. "Yeah. My son can work the counter. Let me prepare your orders first."

In a few minutes, Trish caught Emily's eye and lifted her arms. She had a bagel in one hand and a croissant in the other. Trish jerked her head toward the back of the kitchen, then turned and walked in that direction. Clint was already busy taking a customer's order, and Emily noticed the wary glance he gave Danny.

Emily and Danny followed Trish. When Trish reached the same quiet, out-of-sight corner where Emily and Sage had communicated with Thornton the day before, she turned and handed over the food. "Is this the most casual arrest ever, or do you have good news for me?" Trish asked.

Danny had already taken a big bite of his bagel, and he made a funny wobbling motion with his head while he chewed. Emily wasn't sure if he was trying to answer without speaking, or if it was his way of saying, *Hang on a minute*. After swallowing, he said, "I'm not here for either of those things. I actually have bad news that involves Emily, but Grainy Day is related in a tangential way, too. I figured I should tell both of you."

Emily blinked a few times at Danny. "Bad news? But you seemed pretty upbeat while we were in line. You didn't indicate anything was wrong when we talked on the phone, either."

Danny put a hand on Emily's shoulder. "Remember what I keep telling you: we know you didn't kill Thornton Daley."

"Okay," Emily said slowly.

"Officer Newton admitted he told you about me reviewing your video cameras. We know you never left your house the night Thornton was murdered. There's no way you could have killed him."

Emily crossed her arms impatiently, accidentally squashing her croissant in the process. "But?"

"But, someone is trying to frame you for Thornton's murder."

Emily could only sigh in response to Danny's revelation. She had experienced too many shocking moments in the past week to feel much this time around; it was like her mind had gone numb to all the strange circumstances of Thornton's murder.

There was also a part of Emily that simply wasn't surprised. She had considered before that someone might have been trying to frame her, because they chose to use a Grainy Day box that had clearly been intended for Eternal Rest.

Trish, on the other hand, was much more agitated by the news. "What do you mean? Does someone have it out for Emily?" Trish was staring at Danny, but one of her hands groped toward Emily. When her fingers found purchase on Emily's forearm, Trish clamped down hard, and Emily wondered if Trish was afraid someone was going to swoop in for an attack at any moment.

"We don't think anyone actually holds a grudge against Emily," Danny explained. "Rather, we think she might just be an easy target. Everyone knows, thanks to Thornton's review of Eternal Rest last year, that Emily serves Grainy Day biscuits and that Thornton himself had negative things to say about that."

"He had a lot of negative things to say about the biscuits themselves, too," Trish grumbled.

"Then, the box that delivered the fatal biscuits wound up having Eternal Rest's name on them. Whether that was intentional or just the box the killer happened to grab, we don't know," Danny continued. "It's possible the killer was going to dispose of the box until they realized it was labeled for Eternal Rest, and they jumped at the chance to implicate Emily by stashing it out at the cemetery in hopes it would be found by the police. Add in Vic Oberfeld's editorial, and things start adding up to really make Emily look suspicious, but there's still no proof the killer went into this with the intention of framing anyone. However, we believe the evidence we discovered this morning is a blatant attempt to pin the blame on Emily."

"What evidence?" Emily asked.

"A note. Here, have a look." Danny pulled a piece of paper from his back pocket. It was a photocopy of a typed message on a small white notecard. It read, *Dear Thornton, How about a fresh start, like these fresh-baked biscuits? Really hoping you can join me for breakfast soon, so you can give me a second chance. Regards, Emily Buchanan.*

Emily and Trish groaned in unison. "You weren't kidding about it being a blatant attempt," Emily noted.

"It's typed, which means we can't do a handwriting analysis," Danny said. "What's interesting is where this note was found: it was snagged in a holly bush at Oak Hill Memorial Garden."

Emily took the paper from Danny's hand and read it a second time. "Was it close to where the killer stashed the empty biscuit box?" she asked.

"It wasn't too far away from that spot," Danny said, nodding. "Reed was the one who found it. I made him promise not to tell you, Emily. Sorry I wanted to wait and tell you once we'd had a chance to do a little digging."

Emily wrinkled her nose. "Is that cemetery humor?"

Danny gave a short laugh. "No."

Trish reached over to grab a biscuit off a nearby cooling rack. She started nibbling at it nervously, then paused to ask, "What did you find in your digging?"

"The note is in pristine condition, except for some small snags from the holly leaves. It's not dirty, the paper is still crisp, and it doesn't look like something that's been sitting outside for more than a week."

Emily drew a sharp breath. "It was planted recently?"

Danny nodded grimly. "That's what it looks like. We think someone realized the trail of clues seems to be pointing to you already, so they decided to give things a little boost. They went back to Memorial Garden and planted false evidence sometime in the past few days. After all, it's unlikely we would have overlooked it in our initial search."

"I blame Vic Oberfeld and his stupid editorial for this," Emily mumbled.

"Actually, I blame you," Danny said, no hint of joking in his tone. "If you weren't close to finding out who the real killer is, then I don't think anyone would have felt the need to leave this note. You're hot on someone's trail, and they want to get you—and the police—off it, and quick."

"Vic? Mercedes? Who could it be?" Emily shook her head in frustration.

Danny shrugged. "We don't know yet, but we're working as hard as we can to find out. The person who left the note doesn't know two very important pieces of information: one, that your security cameras prove you were home the night of Thornton's murder, and two, that Thornton's ghost originally accused Trish of his murder. If Thornton had actually seen this note when he was given the biscuits, his ghost likely would have haunted you, Emily, instead of Trish."

Trish's eyes darted between Danny and Emily. "And who told you about Thornton pointing the finger at me?" Her gaze landed on Emily's face, and she said in a stage whisper, "I thought we weren't going to mention that!"

"I didn't say anything about it!" Emily said.

"I saw Sage a few days ago, and she mentioned Thornton kept unplugging appliances and ruining your ingredients, Trish. I put two and two together." Danny smiled politely.

"I guess you are a good detective," Trish said grudgingly.

"Anyway," Danny continued, "that's it. I wanted both of you to know, since the note involves you, Emily, and your biscuits, Trish. I want you both to be cautious. Don't go anywhere alone until we have this sorted out, please."

Emily gave Danny a little salute. "I've got guests every night, and I'll start setting the security alarm when I'm home by myself during the day. Should I call you when I need an escort to go grocery shopping?"

Danny gave Emily a lopsided smile. "I'd be happy to accompany you."

Once Danny said goodbye—after giving yet another warning to both women—and left, Trish and Emily turned and stared at each other.

"Thornton's case is getting a lot more complicated," Trish said.

"Remember when I said I wanted nothing to do with this murder?" Emily chuckled. "So much for that. You know, I was coming here to ask you if I could see a copy of the review Thornton wrote about Grainy Day. Danny meeting me here was a little surprise."

Trish looked confused. "Why do you want to see that review?"

Emily explained her theory to Trish about the connection between the biscuit dough with circles drawn in it and the newspaper article Thornton's ghost kept manipulating. "I can't imagine what other review could have included a photo like that. Who else in town makes biscuits?"

"There aren't many of us, that's for sure," Trish agreed. "Hang on. Let me go rummage through my files. I haven't looked at that review in so long, I can't remember whether that was the photo or not."

Trish's office was a re-purposed closet, barely fitting a small desk, a chair, and a filing cabinet. "Good thing you're petite," Emily remarked as Trish wedged herself into the chair. Emily was hovering in the office doorway, since there wasn't room for two people to fit inside the tiny space.

Trish pulled open a filing cabinet door and started to look quickly through the manila folders inside. Eventually, she said, "Here's my collection of newspaper and magazine clippings about the bakery." Trish opened the folder and began to flip through an impressive stack of articles and photos. Thornton's review of Grainy Day was the very last one, and Trish grimaced as she handed it to Emily. "I, uh, put it on a dart board one night at Sutter's Bar," she admitted.

Emily had to laugh at the tiny holes that peppered the newsprint. Her laugh turned into a sigh when she saw the accompanying photo. It looked nothing like the image Thornton's ghost had drawn in the dough. Instead, the photo showed a basket piled with biscuits, croissants, bagels, and other pastries.

The holes from Trish's darts had obscured a few words of the review, but it was still easy enough to read. Emily scanned the text on the unlikely chance there was something pertinent to Thornton's murder within it. As Trish had already told her, the review focused mostly on Grainy Day's biscuits, and Thornton seemed to have relished describing them as dry and utterly lacking in flavor. *The biscuits would be better,* Thornton had written, *if Mrs. Alden used more butter. My mother wasn't a professional baker, but her biscuits were far superior, thanks to the copious amount of butter she incorporated.*

Emily handed the review back to Trish. "I know I've seen a newspaper photo that looks like the one you took of the dough," Emily said. "If I have to search every single one of Thornton's reviews, I will."

As if in answer, there was a loud smack right behind Emily. She turned and saw the now-familiar frame containing the grand opening announcement lying face-down at her feet.

Emily looked up, startled. "That frame hangs on the opposite wall of the kitchen! Thornton had to throw it a long way to make it all the way over here!"

"Maybe he's telling you that you need to get to the library and start searching," Trish suggested. "Honestly, why can't the guy just write us a nasty review, describing all the ways we're incompetent at finding his killer while suggesting how we could be doing it better? That would be more like Thornton, and it would probably be more helpful."

Emily was staring at the frame, shaking her head. "There's something about this particular article, Trish. Why else would Thornton keep drawing our attention to it? I read the article, I looked at the photo, and I even had Danny look into the writer, but there was nothing that seemed relevant."

Frustrated, Emily reached down and grabbed the hanging wire that ran across the back of the frame. When she tugged on it, the cardboard backing lifted, but the frame stayed put on the floor. "Oh! This was loose in the frame!"

Emily looked down at the frame again, and she

instantly knew the backing hadn't simply come loose. Thornton had moved the tabs holding it in place so Emily would see what was on the backside of the grand opening article.

It was a photo of dough, with perfect rows of circles cut into it.

24

"This is it!" Emily shouted. "This is the photo I remembered!" She glanced up briefly and said warmly, "Oh, thank you, Thornton!"

Emily snatched up the newspaper clipping. The photo was clearly the one she had remembered seeing before, though why it would have stuck in her mind was beyond her. The article it accompanied had been cut short when the Grainy Day grand opening article had been trimmed out of the newspaper, so only the first two paragraphs remained. In them, Thornton stated he had just returned from a restaurant convention, where he had nearly died. *And the cause of my death, had it occurred,* the article stated, *would have been due to a lack of competence.*

"Such a drama queen," Emily mumbled.

The next paragraph was less sensational, as Thornton went on to say the food on display at the convention had been sadly lacking in variety, and he had chosen to skip many an uninventive hamburger in the quest to find something more adventurous. *That nearly proved to be my undoing,* Thornton wrote. The article was clipped just below that line.

"Well, what happened?" Emily asked.

"Are you talking to the newspaper article?" Trish teased. She had squeezed in next to Emily, who was still standing in the office doorway, so she could read the article over Emily's arm.

"I need to go to the library to find the rest. No wonder I remember this photo: this article reads like a soap opera, so I'm sure it stuck in my head when I first saw it."

"Keep me posted on how Thornton almost died!" Trish told Emily the date of the newspaper, saying it was burned into her brain since it had been published on her grand opening day, then gave her a gentle shove. "Don't make me wait longer than I have to! What a cliffhanger!"

Emily didn't argue. She rushed out of the bakery, jumped into her car, and was pulling into the library parking lot just four minutes later. Ten minutes after that, she was sitting down at a table with a microfiche file for the edition of *The Oak Hill Monitor* that held the story. Emily had been so breathless when she requested it the librarian actually asked her if she was okay.

The announcement about the opening of Grainy Day Bakery was on the front page of the local section, so Emily easily found Thornton's article on the backside. She sat hunched over the newspaper, reading the rest of the story as quickly as she could.

After his dramatic opening, Thornton had gone on to explain he had happened upon a restaurant at the convention that was showing off its Asian-inspired dishes. *It looked so enticing: a steaming sticky bun topped with braised beef, pickled vegetables, and just a drizzle of an orange-honey glaze,* Thornton had written.

Emily looked at the photo again, realizing it wasn't biscuits at all, but buns for the beef sandwiches.

I asked if the dish had peanuts in it, Thornton went on. *After all, the legumes are a staple in many an Asian dish. I was assured there were no peanuts in this sandwich, so I bit into it with delight. I confess, it tasted divine, even as my esophagus began to swell and I started to gasp for breath.*

The rest of Thornton's article was a blow-by-blow account of his suffering and how he had to use his EpiPen to prevent himself from dying. It was the final two sentences that really caught Emily's attention: *Clearly, The Golden Lamp does not care about its customers enough to learn what ingredients are in their own dishes. Jackson residents, beware!*

Emily read the sentence again, her excitement rising. *This has to be it. The restaurant name must be what Thornton wanted us to see!*

Emily snapped a photo of the article with her phone, then returned it to the librarian. She decided to take the information straight to Danny, and as she drove, she went through question after question in her mind. Had someone at that restaurant been trying to kill Thornton all those years ago? Had that same person been the one to lace Trish's biscuits with ground peanuts? And how in the world did this tie in to the images of money Thornton's ghost had shown Sage?

If Thornton had already told the story of The Golden Lamp nearly killing him, right there in *The Oak Hill Monitor* for thousands of people to read, then it didn't make sense he would have been receiving money to keep quiet about the incident. So, then, why had Thornton suddenly started getting monthly cash payments, and how did they tie into his near-death experience all those years ago?

Emily felt like her head was buzzing by the time she parked in the small lot behind the Oak Hill Police Department. Instead of going right in, she stayed in her car and called Sage.

Sage said hello, then yawned.

"Did I call right in the middle of your nap?" Emily asked apologetically.

"It's okay. I can tell whatever you have on your mind is more important than a little shut-eye."

Emily told her about the article, and Sage immediately

agreed Thornton was probably indicating The Golden Lamp. "We need to research it," Sage said. "No, you need to research it. Find out everything you can. I'm going straight to the source while you do that."

"You mean you're going to ask Thornton?"

"Exactly. Now that you have a restaurant name and a town—Jackson, you said?—I can ask him some very specific questions. Come on over to the bakery when you're done with your research, and you and I can compare notes."

Emily agreed, then said, "My brain feels like it's overflowing, Sage. What can I do about it?"

"Deep breaths," Sage instructed. "Focus on your goal: finding Thornton's killer. All those questions and details that are swirling around in your brain will slow down. Think of your brain as a dirty puddle of water."

"Ew."

"When you stir it up, the whole thing is muddy. When you stop poking at it with a stick, the dirt will settle to the bottom, and you'll have clear water."

"That kind of makes sense, actually," Emily said. "Thanks, Sage. Good luck!"

This is it, Emily thought as she climbed out of her car. *We're so close! Maybe, just maybe, I can go to bed tonight without this weighing on my brain.*

Emily's excitement came crashing down when she asked for Detective Hernandez at the front desk of the police station and was told he was unavailable. She sat impatiently in an uncomfortable chair in the small waiting area, her legs crossed and one foot tapping away.

While she waited, Emily pulled out her phone and searched for The Golden Lamp online. She did find a listing for a restaurant by that name in Jackson, Mississippi, but instead of seeing its opening hours, there was a line noting it was permanently closed.

It was easy to see why the restaurant had gone out of business: the online reviews were atrocious. Nearly every review began with a statement about the food being great, followed by a "but." *But, the restaurant wasn't very clean. But, the service was slow. But, half of the menu items were unavailable.*

Emily noted wryly there were no reviews about unexpected peanuts.

Before too long, Emily heard her name being called. She glanced up and saw Danny, who looked slightly perplexed. "Come on back to my office," he said. Emily could hear the curiosity in his voice.

Once they were inside Danny's office and the door was shut, he began talking before he was even settled in his chair. "What's going on? Are you okay?"

"I'm fine," Emily said quickly. "Something really interesting happened after you left the bakery!"

When Emily got to the part of her story about The Golden Lamp, explaining her assumption Thornton wanted her to track down whomever had been involved with that restaurant, Danny held up a hand. "You're talking about a restaurant in Mississippi," he cautioned. "By that logic, our killer came all the way to Oak Hill to kill Thornton, then came back a week later to plant false evidence to implicate you in the crime."

"The killer could have stayed here for a while," Emily suggested, even as she realized how silly that sounded.

"What I think is important here is that Thornton admitted he had a deadly peanut allergy in the newspaper. Think about all the Oak Hill residents who have read that article. All of them learned exactly how they could kill Thornton: get him to eat peanuts, and make sure his EpiPen is nowhere to be found."

Emily dropped her face into her hands. "Great, we went from the suspect list including every restaurant and cafe owner in Oak Hill to the entire subscriber list of *The Oak Hill Monitor*."

"Or anyone who read the story on file at the library, like you did," Danny pointed out.

"You're not helping."

Danny leaned forward, his palms spread out flat against the surface of his desk. "I'm not trying to make a joke," he said. "It's been more than a week, and our suspect list keeps growing exponentially. I've never had a case like this. Of course, it's also the first case I've had in which the victim was a public figure who was disliked by seemingly everyone."

Emily leaned forward, too. She folded her arms on the desk and rested her chin on them, her eyes closed. She thought of Sage, probably in the kitchen at Grainy Day at that moment, trying to talk to Thornton. That made her think of the advice Sage had given her, which Emily had appreciated, then completely ignored.

Still your mind. Focus on the goal. We want to find the person who killed Thornton Daley.

"Emily?" Danny sounded a little worried.

"Give me a second. I'm thinking," Emily answered without opening her eyes. She heard the creak of Danny's chair and knew he was leaning back, settling in to let her sort through her thoughts.

Emily took a couple of deep breaths, telling herself over and over again that the goal was to find Thornton's killer. As Sage had promised, she felt her mind slowing down and her thoughts becoming less chaotic.

Yes, Emily realized, Danny made a good point that Thornton's article could be used as a guide to killing him. It seemed pointless, though, for Thornton's ghost to draw attention to that article just to say anyone in town could have done it. Sage had suspected Thornton might not know who had killed him, but he definitely had an idea of who it could have been.

"He wanted me to read that article to make a connection," Emily said quietly. She opened her eyes and sat up straight. "Danny, please indulge me. Let's look into that restaurant in Jackson. I really feel like that's what Thornton wanted me to see."

Danny shrugged affably. "Why not? It's worth a shot."

"I looked online while I was waiting to see you, but the place went out of business," Emily said.

"That doesn't tell us much, does it?" Danny was already turning to his computer. He began typing while Emily tried to wait patiently. Danny started laughing after a few minutes, and he said, "Here's an article from *The Clarion-Ledger*, Jackson's newspaper. Their account of that same convention was very different than Thornton's. According to this article, The Golden Lamp got lots of attention throughout the event, and food critics couldn't stop raving about the braised beef sandwich."

Emily laughed heartily. "The restaurant did get a lot of attention, and Thornton, at least, definitely raved!"

Danny continued typing, then his fingers froze over the keyboard. He stared at the computer screen for a while, and Emily leaned over the desk, trying to see what had caught his attention.

"Huh," Danny said.

"What?"

Danny continued to stare at his screen. "I'm looking at the business license filing for The Golden Lamp. It appears to have been a joint venture between three people. One of them is about to open a restaurant here in Oak Hill: Allen Gerson."

Emily felt lightheaded as Danny's words sank in. Allen Gerson, the man who wanted to serve Trish's murder biscuits at his new barbecue restaurant. Allen, who had invited Emily out to his new place on the edge of town. If Trevor hadn't gone with her, Emily wondered, what might have happened?

Nothing would have happened, Emily told herself, since Mercedes had been there, too. That only brought up a dark possibility. "Allen's new business partner is Mercedes O'Brian," she said. "Do you think she knows? Maybe she was part of it."

"Part of what? Thornton's murder?" Danny asked.

Emily just nodded her head, still reeling.

Danny leaned across the desk and looked at Emily seriously. "Don't jump to conclusions."

She spread her hands. "But it makes sense! If Allen had nearly killed Thornton once before, imagine how mad Thornton must have been when Allen showed up in Oak Hill! He probably threatened to write about the incident and its connection to Allen if he didn't pay him hush money." Emily gasped as another thought struck her. "Allen even told me he had first met Thornton at a food conference in Alabama. It must have been the one mentioned in the articles."

Danny's eyes focused on a spot on his desk, and he bit his lip as he thought. Slowly, almost grudgingly, he said, "Your theory makes some sense, but one accident with peanuts is hardly enough to ruin a restaurant, or to stop one in its tracks before it ever opens. If Allen is our killer, then there must have been some other dirt Thornton had on him."

Emily admitted she didn't know of any other reason Thornton might have had for blackmailing Allen, but Danny was already scribbling in his notebook. "We'll be able to use this article as a reason to look at Allen's financial records," he said, more to himself than to Emily. "We can also talk to him about his past, and we'll dig to see what else Thornton might have had against him."

As Danny continued to write, Emily thought back over the times she had met Allen and the things they had discussed. "Covington," she said abruptly. When Danny looked up at her questioningly, she continued, "Allen told me he had owned a barbecue restaurant in Covington. Maybe that's worth looking into."

Danny nodded and scribbled some more. "He sure has bounced around a lot," he said. "Jackson, Covington, and now, Oak Hill. Usually, restaurant owners rely on their connection to the community to build business. Though, if The Golden Lamp was as bad as the reviews say, I can see why Allen might have wanted a fresh start in some other town."

"Sage is over at Grainy Day right now," Emily said, digging in her purse for her cell phone. "Let me call her so she can ask Thornton's ghost about Allen." Emily stood and started to pace in the tiny area in front of Danny's desk while she waited for Sage to pick up, but the call went to voicemail. Instead of leaving a message, Emily hung up and turned to Danny. "I'm going to head over there since she's not answering."

Danny rose from his chair and came around the side of the desk. "Emily, what have I been telling you since this whole thing started?"

"To stay out of it," Emily said flatly. "But you also said Sage and I could continue to communicate with Thornton's ghost!"

Danny sighed in resignation. "I did. You can go to the bakery, and then I want you to go home. In fact, I'm pretty sure I told you an hour ago not to go anywhere alone, yet here you are, running around town."

Emily felt her cheeks flush. "I know."

"I'm going to ask Allen to come in and have a little chat. Please, don't talk to him before I do. I want to get this sorted out as much as you do, but I'll be a lot happier if I can do it without you putting yourself in a dangerous situation along the way."

Emily raised her right hand. "I promise. You definitely don't have to worry about me trying to question him myself!"

Danny put a hand on Emily's shoulder and looked at her intently. At first, Emily was afraid he was going to revisit whatever subject had been on his lips at the end of his visit to Eternal Rest. Instead, all he said was, "Be careful."

Emily left the police station and drove back to the bakery. She really could have walked, but driving would save her a little time, and she wanted to catch Sage before she wrapped up her session with Thornton and headed back to her office.

When Emily parked and got out of her car, something felt different. As she walked toward the front door of the bakery, she realized what it was. There was no one on the sidewalk near Grainy Day. After the crush of people coming in and out of the bakery in recent days, it was surprising not to see a single person coming out the door with baked goods.

As soon as Emily pulled on the door, she knew why. It was locked.

Emily put her face close to the glass on the door and shaded her eyes with her hands so she could see inside. She didn't see anyone, though the lights were on. It was surprising Trish would close Grainy Day just so Sage could have a séance, especially when Sage had told Emily she didn't need complete silence and isolation to communicate with ghosts. Hoping it meant Sage was really making progress with Thornton, Emily walked quickly down the street and around to the back of the building.

The back door of the bakery was cracked open, and as Emily got closer, she slowed her pace and tried to be as quiet as possible so she wouldn't interrupt Sage. Emily stopped just outside the door and leaned forward, pressing one ear into the narrow gap between the door and the doorframe.

Emily had expected to hear Sage's voice. Instead, she heard a man speaking.

"You're not telling me everything you know," the man said insistently.

"What does it matter to you?" Emily recognized Trish's voice, and even though Trish was speaking in a sharp tone, Emily could hear her underlying fear.

"Thornton Daley didn't like me much," continued the man. "If his ghost is here, it might be saying some things about me that aren't true."

Emily's mouth opened in surprise as she recognized the voice. It was Allen Gerson.

The next voice that spoke was clearly Sage's. "Thornton doesn't actually know who killed him, so you don't need to worry he's going to point the finger at you."

There was a pause, then Allen spoke again. His voice was louder this time, his anger increasing. "You're lying!"

Someone—Emily couldn't tell whether it was Trish or Sage—squeaked out a little scream.

"I want to know every single thing Thornton has told you, and then, maybe, I'll let you live," Allen continued. "Do you understand?"

Emily brought both hands up to stifle the cry she felt rising in her throat. Quickly but quietly, she shuffled sideways until her body was no longer visible through the door. She turned, pressing her back against the building as she wondered what to do.

If Allen had already killed Thornton, then Emily knew his threat to Sage and Trish wasn't just posturing. He must have heard the gossip that Thornton's ghost was haunting Grainy Day, and he was trying to cut off communication between the living and the dead.

You're too late, Allen, Emily thought, even as she reached into her purse to retrieve her cell phone. She felt glued to the side of the building, too frightened to run away, but she knew she had to alert the police. If she called nine one one, Allen might hear her voice. Instead, she texted Danny. The first text she sent simply read, *He's here!*

Emily was typing a more detailed message to tell Danny exactly who was where when she heard a metallic squeal. Emily glanced up, her heart pounding, and saw the back door of the bakery opening wider. Soon, Allen's white cowboy hat appeared as he leaned through the doorway.

Allen stared at Emily for a long time, and she finally mustered the courage to say, "I'm here to see Trish." She was hoping Allen would believe she had just arrived, but she could hear the way her voice shook and knew Allen wouldn't buy it. It was obvious she had overheard him threatening her friends.

"You know," Allen said, as if he and Emily were having

a casual conversation, "I'm glad you're here. I was just thinking about how to solve a little problem of mine, and now I've realized you're the solution I was looking for."

Allen's arm shot out, and he snatched Emily's phone out of her hand. He quickly threw it away from her, and Emily heard it skittering across the asphalt of the parking lot. Without pausing, Allen grabbed Emily's wrist and pulled, yanking her toward him. Before she crashed into his chest, Allen released her wrist and pushed hard against the back of Emily's shoulder, shoving her through the doorway and into the bakery.

Emily stumbled to a halt. She felt a brief moment of relief when she saw both Trish and Sage appeared unhurt, but they were cowering, arms around each other and their backs pressed against a countertop. The next emotion Emily felt was something like annoyance as she wondered why one of them hadn't seized the opportunity to dash out the front door while Allen had been dealing with Emily.

There was motion to the left side of Emily's face, and out of the corner of her eye, she saw that Allen had a gun trained on Sage and Trish. He had put his gun in his left hand so he could keep his aim on them while he had dealt with Emily. He stood close behind Emily, his arm stretched over her shoulder and his gun still aimed right at her friends.

No wonder they couldn't make a run for it. But I could step on his foot and knock the gun out of his hand! Emily thought wildly. But, no, she told herself, there was too much of a risk he would fire and hit Sage or Trish.

"You," Allen said calmly, "are going to be blamed for the murder of these two women. How unfortunate for you. The story will come out that Thornton's ghost told these ladies you had killed him, so you couldn't let them live. I just so happened to come upon the scene right after you shot them. Caught in the act, you panicked and fired two shots at me. I had to defend myself, of course. I don't know what foods you're allergic to, so I guess I'll have to find some other way of killing you. I'll tell the police I just meant to hinder you, not kill you. They'll pat me on the back and say I did what I had to do, and then I'll be hailed as the hero who caught Thornton Daley's killer. Imagine how great this will be for my restaurant! Everyone in town will flock to the place."

Emily stood rigidly during Allen's speech, too terrified that any move she made would make him start shooting. Her eyes met Sage's, and Emily was surprised to feel a sense of calm emanating from her best friend. As Allen described his dream of a booming restaurant, Emily thought she even saw the corners of Sage's mouth turn up, ever so slightly.

Just as Emily was wondering what Sage could possibly be happy about, every single frame hanging on the kitchen wall was yanked downward by invisible hands, the sound of shattering glass echoing through the kitchen. At the same time, there was a loud cracking noise directly behind Emily.

Something hit Emily hard in the back of the head, and she lost consciousness as her body fell forward.

26

Emily didn't know how long she had been lying on the cold tile floor of Trish's kitchen when she woke up, blinking her eyes slowly and feeling pain flare in the back of her head. She tried to move, then realized something heavy was holding her down. She craned her head around, expecting to see Allen restraining her. Instead, she only saw a limp arm that obscured her vision.

A woman was crying hysterically somewhere above Emily, occasionally wailing, "I'm sorry! I'm so sorry!"

There was another sound, a squeak which Emily recognized as the back door. Then a man said kindly but urgently, "Ma'am, put it down. It's okay. It's okay. Come with me."

Emily recognized Danny's voice, and even though she was pinned to the ground, she felt her body relax. Danny had seen and understood her text message, which meant she and her friends were out of danger.

"Hang on, Em, we're going to get you up," Sage said. There was some grunting, then Emily felt the weight roll off her back. She twisted her body around to find herself lying next to the prone form of Allen Gerson. He had a bloody nose, and his cowboy hat was missing.

On her other side, Sage and Trish stood together.

"That dude is heavy!" Trish said. Her hair was disheveled, and her hands were shaking.

Emily stood up slowly, mindful of her aching skull. Sage caught her under the arms and pulled her into a tight hug. "You okay?" Sage asked.

"Allen hit me in the head," Emily said, rubbing a hand over the knot she felt forming.

Sage released Emily and laughed. "Yeah, with his face! Mercedes whacked him in the back of the head with a baseball bat, then he crashed into you." Sage nodded toward Allen, who was just beginning to wake up as the police rolled him over to put him in handcuffs. "I think he broke his nose on your noggin."

"Gross." Emily reached a hand back again and rubbed her hair. It wasn't wet, and she was relieved Allen hadn't bled on her. "Wait, you said Mercedes hit him?"

Emily didn't have to look to know that was who had been crying hysterically. Now that her thoughts were more clear, she recognized the sound from Thornton's funeral. The crying was still going, coming from outside, and Emily looked through the open doorway to see Mercedes talking and gesturing wildly to Danny.

"Mercedes was pretty great," Trish said. "Allen had left the door open behind him, and suddenly, bang! He just went down like a chopped tree. She was standing there in the doorway with a baseball bat like some kind of warrior woman."

Emily smiled wanly. "I'll thank her later for saving our lives. Who was she apologizing to, anyway?"

"She seemed to be talking to all of us, including Allen," Sage said. "I'm as eager as you to find out what prompted her to take out her own business partner."

"You knew she was coming, didn't you?" Emily asked. "You suddenly looked pleased about something."

"I didn't know it would be Mercedes," Sage said. Allen

was being helped up from the floor, and he was moaning so loudly Sage stopped talking. She crossed her arms impatiently and glared at Allen until the police had taken him outside before she continued. "Thornton suddenly channeled a message to me that help had arrived. I actually expected the police, not a platinum blonde with a bat."

"It's my fault he knew you were outside, Emily," Trish said apologetically. "I saw you looking through the gap in the door, and I guess he could tell from my expression someone was behind him. Hang on, I'll go get some ice out of the freezer for your head."

While Trish busied herself making an ice pack, Emily turned to Sage and asked, "What did I miss? And why was the bakery closed in the middle of the day?"

"Allen came in through the back door while I was trying to communicate with Thornton. I knew something was wrong just before he walked in, because Thornton started channeling a feeling of danger to me. It was so strong I actually got up off the floor and was about to grab Trish so we could make a run for it. But, it was too late. He had a gun in his hand, and he kept it down by his side so the customers couldn't see it. He told Trish to get everyone out and lock up, then he started asking us what Thornton had told us."

"I was over at the police station just before I came here. Danny and I had figured out Allen was the likely culprit, thanks to Thornton's hints, but we still don't know what could have prompted Allen to kill him."

Sage began to respond when there was a loud shout, and Emily turned to see Clint rushing into the kitchen. "Mom! Mom, are you okay?" He ran to Trish and grasped her arms, giving her a searching look.

"I'm fine. This ice pack is for Emily, not me."

Clint whirled around to Emily. "What happened? The police are hauling a guy away, and there's a lady crying out in the parking lot. I just went to the store! I thought Mom would be safe while I was gone! What did the ghost do this time?"

Trish handed Emily a handful of ice wrapped in a towel, then put a comforting arm around Clint's shoulders. "The ghost didn't do anything; a living person did this. We'll fill you in shortly, but in the meantime, just know that we're okay," she assured her son.

"Actually, I can fill you in right now." Danny was walking up to the group, and he stopped next to Emily, who hissed in her breath as she put the ice pack against the bump on her head. "Are you badly hurt?"

"No. Allen got the worst of it."

Despite Emily's reassurance, Danny made her move the ice pack so he could inspect the growing knot on the back of her head. "It doesn't look terrible," he mumbled, but he looked at Emily worriedly before turning his attention to everyone in the group.

"Allen started confessing before we even got him in the squad car," Danny said. "Thornton was blackmailing him, as we had speculated. When Thornton found out Allen had moved to Oak Hill and wanted to open a barbecue restaurant here, he started looking into Allen's history. Apparently, Thornton wanted to see if anyone else with food allergies had gotten into trouble at The Golden Lamp. Instead, what Thornton found was a string of failed restaurants, lots of reports of code violations and bad service, and a history of skipping town without paying the bills."

Sage snorted. "Thornton himself wasn't so good at paying the bills, according to Mercedes."

"Thornton threatened to expose Allen's past," Danny continued. "Allen started making the monthly payments to keep Thornton quiet, but he quickly realized he couldn't afford to keep it up indefinitely. Instead of coming to the police, like he should have, he killed Thornton."

"And tried to frame me for the murder," Emily added.

"We haven't confirmed that yet, but we'll certainly ask him." Danny shook his head. "And here I thought you would be safe just talking to a ghost."

Trish leaned back against the counter, a satisfied little smile on her face. "Just wait 'til everyone hears about this! I'm going to need to hire a second baker to keep up with demand."

Sage nodded. "This is going to be good for my business, too."

Danny sighed dramatically. "I'm so glad you ladies have your priorities straight."

Emily heard footsteps behind her, and she turned to see Roger Newton looking at her with the same concern Danny had shown. "Miss Emily, will you please come with me? Danny, you should come, too. You need to hear this."

Emily and Sage exchanged confused glances, then Emily and Danny followed Roger out the door. He walked over to Mercedes, who had stopped crying but was still sniffing loudly while dabbing at her eyes with a tissue. A police officer stood next to her, and Mercedes was holding his arm to steady herself.

"Detective Hernandez, turn on your tape recorder," Roger said. "Ms. O'Brian would like to say something to you, Miss Emily."

Emily stared at Mercedes in surprise, noticing the woman looked even worse than she had at Thornton's funeral. Her eyes were red and puffy, and her bun was falling apart. As Emily watched, Mercedes reached back and tugged at her hair nervously, and a few more strands pulled out of the bun.

"Oh, Emily," Mercedes began, then stopped abruptly. Her face crumpled, and she bit her lip. "I'm so, so sorry.

On Sunday, after you and your friend left the barbecue restaurant, Allen told me he was just making up that story about the place being haunted. He just wanted publicity, and he thought a ghost story combined with selling those biscuits that killed Thornton would be good for business."

Mercedes paused again, and she rubbed her eyes, which only made her eye makeup more of a mess. "I mentioned the rumor about Thornton haunting the bakery where the biscuits had come from, and he got really upset. His face turned red, and he just ranted about how ridiculous it was. I didn't understand his reaction, but on Monday, when we met to go over financials for the restaurant, he said something about having more money at his disposal now. I asked him what he meant, and he said a money problem had been taken care of. There was just something about the way he said it, you know? Then I started thinking back, and I remembered he and I were supposed to meet with a graphic design firm one morning last week, but he never showed up. I couldn't reach Allen by phone, and finally, hours later, he called me back, saying he had overslept. That meeting was scheduled on the morning Thornton's body was found."

"Why didn't you call to report your suspicions?" Danny asked.

"Because they were just that, suspicions." Mercedes ran a hand across her forehead. "Plus, it's been my dream for years to have a restaurant. Teaming up with Allen was my last chance. If this place failed, I'd never be able to save up enough money to try again. I didn't want to put the restaurant in jeopardy, so I kept quiet."

"He was going to kill us," Emily said quietly. She could understand Mercedes wanting to protect her dream, but it could have come at a steep price.

"I know. This morning, Allen asked me what a good time might be to come here. He said he wanted to talk to

Trish about serving her biscuits at the restaurant, but he didn't want to drop in when the bakery might be really busy with customers. I suggested late afternoon, since I know this place gets a lot of breakfast and lunch business. Again, though, there was just something about the way he said it. After he left the restaurant to come here, I kept worrying, but I still didn't want to call the police. So, finally, I came here myself. I keep the baseball bat in my car, in case I need it for self-defense. I never thought I'd wind up using it on my own partner. I'm so sorry, Emily."

"I'm glad you came," Emily said. "You saved our lives. But, why are you apologizing to me? I think Trish and Sage are the ones who really deserve an apology. They're the ones Allen interrogated at gunpoint."

Mercedes drew in a deep breath, and tears began to run down her face. She looked at Danny, then turned to Emily again. "I'm apologizing to you because I'm the one who tried to frame you for Thornton's murder."

27

Danny stepped closer to Mercedes while extending the hand that held his tape recorder. "You just said you didn't know for sure Allen had killed Thornton," he asked, "so how could you have been Allen's accomplice?"

Mercedes waved her hands wildly. "No, no, no!" she said in rapid-fire delivery. "I wasn't his accomplice. But I knew if I thought Allen seemed guilty, then the police would, too. Like I said, I was terrified of anything getting in the way of opening this restaurant. Then, I read that editorial in the paper, where Vic Oberfeld made Emily look guilty. I thought planting a note from Emily might keep the police looking at her rather than at Allen." Mercedes pressed her hands against her chest. Her eyes dropped to the ground as she addressed Emily again. "I'm sorry. It was so selfish of me. I could have ruined your life, just so I could have my dream of helping run a restaurant."

Emily wasn't sure how to react to Mercedes's confession. Part of her was incredibly angry and wanted to yell in her face, but another part of her felt pity. After everything she had been through with Thornton and the aftermath of their failed partnership, Mercedes had acted like the desperate woman she was.

I'll have to ask Trevor how he managed to forgive his father. Maybe he can help me learn to forgive Mercedes.

When Emily didn't say anything, Danny continued questioning Mercedes. "If you weren't Allen's accomplice, then how did you know the box of biscuits he gave Thornton had been earmarked for Eternal Rest and made Emily look suspicious?"

"What? I didn't know," Mercedes said, shaking her head.

Danny turned to Emily. "If Mercedes was the one trying to frame you, that means Allen probably grabbed a random box out of Trish's car, and it was just a coincidence it was the one labeled for you."

"I didn't meet Allen until after Thornton's death, so that makes more sense than him framing me from the start," Emily said.

"Rest assured, I'll still ask him about it."

Emily just nodded. Danny's voice seemed to be coming from far away. Emily's body was beginning to ache from being thrown to the floor, and the knot on her head throbbed. Between the pain of Allen hitting her and the whirlwind of thoughts in her mind, Emily felt like her skull was going to crack open. Suddenly, she felt weary. She wanted to simply climb into her car and drive away from all this.

"We'll have more questions for you at the police station," Danny said to Mercedes.

"Wait," Emily said, putting a hand on Danny's arm to stop him from guiding Mercedes to a nearby patrol car. "Mercedes, why are you telling me that you planted the note? Why not let Allen take the blame for that?"

Mercedes shrugged slowly. "How many people might have died, all because I wanted to open a restaurant? Telling the truth is what I should have done the moment I began to suspect Allen."

Emily gave Mercedes a short nod and turned away as Danny led her to the backseat of the patrol car. Emily walked back into the kitchen, but before she could tell Sage, Trish, and Clint what Mercedes had just confessed, Sage turned her face toward the ceiling and shouted in an exasperated tone, "Not even a thank you?"

"You talking to Thornton?" Emily asked.

"He just left. His killer has been caught, and so he just crossed over without so much as a 'hey, thanks for taking time out of your busy schedule to help me.'"

Trish grumbled, "An apology for ruining all my ingredients would have been nice, too."

Sage looked at Emily, her eyes narrowed. "You were right about Mercedes having a rusty-looking aura, but yours is looking muddy. You need to go home and rest, and I order you to think happy thoughts."

"I do want to go home," Emily agreed. Then she yelped. "Home! Oh, no, what time is it? My poor guests!" Emily looked around wildly. "Where is my phone?"

"Somewhere in the parking lot," Trish reminded her.

With a frustrated groan, Emily turned and went outside. She didn't immediately see her phone on the ground, so she crouched down to peer under the nearest cars. Finally, she located it under a truck, next to the rear tire, and she awkwardly reached under the truck to retrieve it.

The screen was cracked in multiple places, but she could still read it. There were no new messages, which hopefully meant her guests hadn't returned yet to find a locked front door.

After standing still for a moment to let her heart return to its normal pace, Emily found Danny. "I need to go home," Emily said to him.

"Are you sure you don't need to go to the hospital to get your head looked at?" he asked.

"I need to go home," she repeated. "I have guests."

"Okay," Danny agreed reluctantly. "But tomorrow morning, after your guests head out for the day, you're going to the police station to go on record about what happened here today."

"You can have an everything bagel with cream cheese waiting for me." Emily smiled weakly at Danny, waved to Roger, then said a hasty goodbye to Sage, Trish, and Clint.

"I'll see you tomorrow," Sage said.

Emily was too tired to even ask where or when Sage expected to see her.

Emily's doorbell rang at fifteen minutes after five the next afternoon. She had spent most of the day in bed, trying to recover from the physical and mental ordeal she had been through the day before. She was feeling a little better, though her body was stiff and sore from the fall, as she opened the door to see Reed. He had a cooler in his hand.

"That old grill behind your house still works, right?" he asked, not even bothering to say hello.

"I assume so," Emily said, mystified. She glanced at the cooler. "Did you come here to borrow my grill?"

Reed grinned at Emily wickedly. "I thought I'd barbecue for everyone tonight, since Allen won't be opening his restaurant, after all."

Emily snickered, then raised an eyebrow. "Everyone?"

"Don't worry. I've assigned each person to bring something, so you don't need to do a thing. We even included your guests in the planning."

Emily nodded knowingly. "When they came back to the house this afternoon, they were awfully cagey about their plans for dinner tonight. I assume you waylaid them when I wasn't looking?"

Reed straightened his shoulders proudly. "I sure did. The grass outside the cemetery wall needed trimming, so we were close enough to keep a lookout for your guests. I told them the plan as they were heading out for the day."

Two cars were pulling into the circular driveway of Eternal Rest as Emily stood back to let Reed in. Soon, Sage, Jen, and Trevor were on her porch, all bearing shopping bags.

"I brought wine from that local winery I introduced you to," Trevor said.

"And we brought a couple of side dishes," Jen added.

"Thanks, y'all. Now we just need dessert," Emily said, reaching forward to take a bag out of Sage's hands.

"Oh, it's on the way," Jen said confidently as she and Sage went inside and headed straight for the kitchen.

Once it was just Trevor and Emily on the front porch, he looked at her keenly. "Are you feeling okay? It sounds like you might have gotten a concussion yesterday."

"No, just a big lump on the back of my head. Honestly, my brain hurts more than my body. I still can't believe Mercedes tried to frame me for Thornton's murder, all so she could help open a barbecue restaurant."

Trevor smiled sadly. "People do crazy things to protect their dreams."

"Yeah."

"I'm disappointed I didn't get to help as much this time around, but I'm proud of you for figuring it out."

"Thanks. And you helped a lot! If it weren't for you talking me into going to Thornton's funeral, I wouldn't have even known who Mercedes O'Brian was, let alone that she was in business with our killer." Emily shivered and rubbed her arms briskly. "And, if I hadn't met Mercedes, she might not have shown up at Grainy Day in time to save my life. And Sage's and Trish's lives, for that matter."

Trevor put an arm around Emily's shoulders and steered her toward the front door. "Can you believe my dad's funeral was only a week ago yesterday?"

"It's been a long week."

"Yeah. Come on, let's crack into this wine. We've earned it."

Emily and Trevor loaded glasses of wine onto a couple of trays and took them to the backyard, where everyone was gathered around the grill as Reed tended to the chicken and pork. Even Emily's guests were there, chatting easily with the group and soaking in every detail of Thornton's murder and their hostess's role in finding his killer. The day was still hot, but as the sun dipped below the tallest trees in Hilltop Cemetery, a light breeze picked up. Emily looked around happily, enjoying the nice evening and the company. Scott had always been the one who did the grilling, but Emily told herself she would start hosting cookouts for her friends and her guests on a regular basis.

Reed was just taking the first items off the grill when Trish came walking around the side of the house, a big basket in her hand. "Dessert is here!" she announced grandly.

"Don't tell me you brought murder biscuits!" Emily teased.

"I did, actually, but they're for dinner. For dessert, I brought a cherry pie, a chess pie, and—for our gluten-free guest—a flourless torte." Trish began to unload the items from her basket onto a folding table Sage and Jen had set up to hold the food. Emily joined her, helping rearrange everything to make space for the desserts.

"Allen stood there and watched him eat the biscuits, you know," Trish said quietly to Emily.

"Really? Danny didn't mention it when I went to the police station to give my statement this morning." Emily glanced around. "Why isn't he here, anyway?"

Trish looked slightly embarrassed. "I asked Sage not to invite him. I'll eventually get over him suspecting me of murder, but it's still a little too fresh in my mind. I don't want to grill out with a guy who grilled me for a solid hour!"

Emily snickered, then quickly turned serious again. "Allen actually watched Thornton die?"

"Allen said he asked Thornton to meet him at his new restaurant, claiming he had the latest blackmail payment for him. When Thornton showed up, Allen handed him the cash, then told him he was planning to serve my biscuits. He told Thornton I had made up a special recipe just for the restaurant, and I had specifically asked for Thornton's opinion of them, in case I needed to tweak the recipe." Trish gave a little shrug. "No wonder his ghost haunted me instead of Allen. In fact, Allen admitted he planted the biscuit box there at the cemetery, hoping to make me look guilty. So, he wasn't trying to frame you at all."

"If it hadn't been for Thornton's ghost, Allen would probably have gotten away with it," Emily said incredulously. "Since the restaurant is a little way out of town, I bet no one saw Allen dragging Thornton's body to his truck so he could dump it at the cemetery." Emily shook her head in disgust.

"Exactly. Funny enough, it was Reed's team who foiled Allen's plans to bury Thornton at the cemetery. They arrived at Memorial Garden early to prepare for Trevor's dad's funeral, and Allen had to run off before he'd finished the job."

"How ironic that a murderer's funeral got in the way of another murderer's work."

Trish glanced over her shoulder. "I'll let you tell Trevor, if you think he'll take it well."

"I think he'll appreciate it, actually." Emily looked in

the same direction as Trish and saw Trevor talking animatedly with two of her guests. Beyond them, Sage was standing slightly apart from everyone else, staring toward Hilltop Cemetery. Her arms hung limp at her sides, the last drops of wine spilling out from the glass she was still holding loosely in her fingers.

"Hang on," Emily said distractedly to Trish. She hurried over to Sage, but instead of looking at her friend, she peered toward Hilltop, too. "What do you sense?"

"It's what I see," Sage said quietly. "In the past few minutes, I've seen three ghosts. They all seem to be traveling from somewhere on the other side of the cemetery, and they are all going in the direction of downtown Oak Hill."

"Was Scott one of them?" Emily asked hopefully.

When Sage didn't answer, Emily turned and looked at her. Sage leaned forward slightly, still staring at the cemetery. "No, he wasn't one of them, but I can sense him, Emily! I can feel him there, just outside the barrier."

"That's wonderful! He's getting stronger! I'm going to go up the hill to look for him."

Sage nodded, then shook her head. "Yes, you should, but I don't think he's getting stronger. We've been making that assumption since you saw him, especially since Kelly says he's looking better and brighter at every sighting. But I don't think that's what's happening. Rather, I think the psychic barrier around Oak Hill is getting weaker, so we're better able to see Scott."

"Well," Emily said, fighting her disappointment. "That's good news, too. If the barrier is weakening, maybe Scott will be able to get past it soon and come home."

"Maybe. The question is, why are so many other ghosts flocking to Oak Hill? What's drawing them here?"

"I have no idea, but I think you're about to be a very busy woman."

A NOTE FROM THE AUTHOR

Raise your hand if you've got a craving for biscuits right now! Thank you for continuing to be on this journey with Emily, Sage, and the rest of the Eternal Rest gang. Will you please leave a review for this book on Amazon or your favorite book review site? It helps other paranormal cozy readers find their next book, and it helps me continue to tell stories.

Thank you,

Beth

NEXT IN THE SERIES

Find out what's next for Emily, Sage, and the ghosts of Eternal Rest Bed and Breakfast!

ETERNAL REST BED AND BREAKFAST BOOK SIX
PARANORMAL COZY MYSTERIES

Guests are bringing magic and murder to Eternal Rest Bed and Breakfast.

Emily Buchanan believes in ghosts but not in witches. Her skepticism turns to shock when Eternal Rest Bed and Breakfast hosts a witches' weekend, and she learns a truth that will reframe the past two years of her life. Emily will never look at her life or her late husband, Scott, in the same way again.

But when one of the witches turns up dead, Emily suddenly has a houseful of suspects, and every one of them is pointing their wand at someone else. Emily must navigate personal agendas, bitter rivalries, and astonishing revelations to find the real killer.

Meanwhile, Scott's ghost is in a race against time. If Emily is going to help him, it must be soon. She will need the help of her best friend, Sage, as well as her own blossoming psychic medium skills to bring his ghost home to Eternal Rest before it's too late...

BOOKS BY BETH DOLGNER

The Eternal Rest Bed and Breakfast Series
Paranormal Cozy Mystery
Sweet Dreams
Late Checkout
Picture Perfect
Scenic Views
Breakfast Included
Groups Welcome
Quiet Nights

The Nightmare, Arizona Series
Paranormal Cozy Mystery
Homicide at the Haunted House
Drowning at the Diner
Slaying at the Saloon
Murder at the Motel
Poisoning at the Party
Clawing at the Corral

The Betty Boo, Ghost Hunter Series
Romantic Urban Fantasy
Ghost of a Threat
Ghost of a Whisper
Ghost of a Memory
Ghost of a Hope

Manifest
Young Adult Steampunk
A Talent for Death
Young Adult Urban Fantasy

Nonfiction
Georgia Spirits and Specters
Everyday Voodoo

ABOUT THE AUTHOR

Beth Dolgner writes paranormal fiction and nonfiction. Her interest in things that go bump in the night really took off on a trip to Savannah, Georgia, so it's fitting that her first series—Betty Boo, Ghost Hunter—takes place in that spooky city. Beth also writes paranormal nonfiction, including her first book, *Georgia Spirits and Specters*, which is a collection of Georgia ghost stories.

Beth and her husband, Ed, live in Tucson, Arizona. Their Victorian bungalow is possibly haunted, but it's not nearly as exciting as the ghostly activity at Eternal Rest Bed and Breakfast.

Beth also enjoys giving presentations on Victorian death and mourning traditions as well as Victorian Spiritualism. She has been a volunteer at an historic cemetery, a ghost tour guide, and a paranormal investigator. Beth likes to think of it all as research for her books.

Keep up with Beth and sign up for her newsletter at
BethDolgner.com

Manufactured by Amazon.ca
Bolton, ON

45068858R00120